THE GOMPA OASIS

Jesse S. Smith

Basementia Publications
Silverton, Oregon

The Gompa Oasis
Jesse S. Smith
Copyright ©2020 by Jesse S. Smith.

Published by Basementia Publications
Silverton, Oregon
www.basementia.com

ISBN 978-0-9766423-3-6

Cover design by Jesse S. Smith
Photos of Vijayanagar Ruins in Hampi, India by Jesse S. Smith
Photo of Grand Canyon by Jesse S. Smith

Typeset in Gentium Book Basic

Science Fiction / Fantasy

*To my sister, Lindsey
for all the adventures*

Author's Note

Inspired by *The Hitchhiker's Guide to the Galaxy, Dune,* and sheer youthful exuberance, I wrote the original version of this zany otherworld story in sporadic sessions from the summer of 1996 through January of 1998: my senior year of college, and the year that followed.

Then I shelved the project for more than 20 years.

I returned to it in October of 2019 for an extensive overhaul. This was a fun project to return to, because the writing style is so lighthearted.

I hope you will enjoy reading it as much as I enjoyed creating it.

-J.S.
August 23, 2020

Chapter 1: The Students

The sun had just disappeared behind the distant mountains when a large enclosed wagon, pulled by a long black reptilian creature with three pairs of legs, drove up to the ancient ruins.

Upon reaching the landmark, a door opened in the side of the wagon, and out sprang a young adult male humanoid figure with a small bucket in one hand. He eagerly jumped down to the ground before the vehicle had even ceased its movement; but he landed at slightly the wrong angle, and ended up face down in the sand.

This accident did not stop him. He popped back up in a moment and ran at full tilt to the far end of the ruins, where stood a raised brick terrace with a well in its center.

Behind him, the driver steered the six-legged dromi by its sturdy reins down the empty deserted streets of the ancient stone ruins with their eerie wind-worn carvings.

The first traveler was already inspecting the well at the center of the sand-covered plaza ruins.

"Hey, Sriaugh!" the traveler called back over his shoulder to the driver in excitement, "there's water in this one!"

The expression of relief which crossed the driver's face attested to the fact that there had not been water in the last well they had visited; nor in the one before that.

"That's great, Gantsch. Do you see any dead things floating in it?" Sriaugh queried anxiously, as he clambered stiffly down from his seat and made his travel-weary descent from the carriage.

"Nope," said Gantsch with palpable relief, "I do not see any dead floaty things. In fact," he noted as he threw down his bucket and hauled it back up by the rope, "this water is remarkably cool and clear." This was a pleasant change.

Here, crossing the deep sand of the uninhabited Northern Plain of the Zensai Desert, water was scarce. The cracked and rubble-strewn road they traveled was a long straight line across the flattest, most arid desert of the whole Mohaani Peninsula. There were sometimes clouds, and occasionally even visible rain, high in the sky; but the rain always evaporated before ever it reached the dusty ground. Consequently, most of the water they had found along their journey was warm and silty. Even when there were no visible dead things floating in the water, there was often some rather questionable slime growing near it. Neither filtering nor boiling could completely remove the taste. And then there had been the dry wells. After all that, this latest well seemed too good to be true.

Gantsch knew from his University classes that the Imperial seat of the entire region had once been in this part of the country; but it was all destroyed in the Fire Wars, long ago. What hadn't been pulverized into its component molecules back then was now buried under huge sand dunes. These ancient ruins with their old stone well were a strange exception. It might be fortuitous to examine them in more detail, just to satisfy his curiosity.

"What do you say we camp here for the night?" Gantsch proposed.

"Yeah, I was just thinking the same thing, myself," Sriaugh readily assented.

*   *   *

Recent graduation from the university in the populous port city of Varum had left Gantsch with some free time and unprecedented freedom to choose the next direction in his life. Without any pressing engagements, he was taking his time returning home, and traveling the ancient Imperial Highway across the broad sandy plans of the Zensai Desert. For the journey, Gantsch had caught a ride with his school drinking buddy, Sriaugh, who conveniently owned his own dromi-wagon.

"Isn't the crossing dangerous?" Gantsch had asked with a certain amount of trepidation. "I thought the desert has man-eating monsters."

"What, the gargathods?" Sriaugh had replied with a note of scorn in his voice. "Well, maybe, but nah. They're only dangerous if you don't know how to avoid them, because they're really incredibly stupid."

"How do you avoid them?"

"Don't step on one."

Sriaugh's bravado had inspired confidence in the coastal city, where solar stills desalinate sea water to provide the population with an infinite supply of purified drinking water. However, out here in the desert, their partnership had nearly proven disastrous already.

"No problem," Sriaugh had said optimistically, the first time they visited a well that turned out to be empty. "There will be water in the next one."

At the time, shaking his own water bottle doubtfully, Gantsch had reasoned that Sriaugh had made this journey before, whereas he himself had not; so he accepted his friend's guidance without question. There were other jugs, water enough for two more days' journey; so there was no cause for concern.

The next well had turned out to be empty, also.

"Let's press on," Sriaugh had insisted. "I'm sure there's water in the next one."

"You said that about the last one," Gantsch had said reprovingly.

"Sorry," Sriaugh had chuckled carelessly, "my mistake. It's the next one, I'm sure, I'm sure. I just, like, forgot about this one."

"Okaaay," Gantsch had said, feeling doubtful, but too polite to question his friend's guidance. "But we only have enough water for one more day. If there's not water at the next well, we're way out here in the middle of the desert with no water."

"The wells are sometimes finicky this time of year," Sriaugh had admitted, "but there's more moisture than you might think, if you look in the right places. The Dimpai tribes have been wandering around out here for generations, herding their besnouted vebuthas, so you know there's water somewhere, it's just, not always easy to find, but we'll find it. Don't worry."

Despite this hopeful guidance, Gantsch had indeed begun to worry when the vacationing pair reached the third well and found that it, too, was filled with nothing but sand.

"Wait, wait, wait, wait, wait," said Sriaugh then in disbelief.

"Should we try and dig it out?" Gantsch had asked.

"No..." Sriaugh had sighed, and added thoughtfully, "people wouldn't have let it fill up like that if there was water."

Sriaugh was actually a nickname, which could best be translated as "a speedy slide down a steep embankment." He certainly seemed to be earning the moniker, now that the two were out in the middle of the desert with no water, just as Gantsch had feared.

"I think we should go back," Gantsch had said cautiously.

"We can't go back," Sriaugh had protested. "We already know there are two empty wells back in that direction. But if we keep going, we'll reach the next one well before nightfall, and chances are, there will be water in that one."

Gantsch did not like those chances; but he had to admit, they were more likely to find water in the next well than to find water in the previous well.

By the time they had reached this present well, they were desperate enough that even if it had been dirty, silty water; even if it had been slimy with ooze, smelling like shit; even if it had to be squeezed from the moist mud at the bottom of a nearly-dry well: they still would have drank it anyway, because they had no choice.

As it was, they were fortunate, indeed: for they had found the well full of clear-ish water, and it didn't even taste all that funky. The two young men offered their praises to the Sandstorm Gods as they drank deeply from the well at the ruins, and filled up all their water jugs and containers. Then they watered the dromi, and took a stroll around the ruins.

The ancient stone ruins where they had stopped for water were all that then remained of what had once been a roadside rest stop, a part of a system of travelers' amenities established by some forgotten king in the prosperous days of the Empire, before the Fire Wars.

Like all of the ornate place markers along the ancient Imperial Highway from Varum to Kiranesh, this rest stop must once have resembled a small palace at the time of its construction; although centuries of vandalism, disuse and erosion had left only an engraved, crumbling, roofless shell which merely hinted at its former grandeur. Gantsch wandered from room to room, admiring the intricately carved stone-masonry. He could afford to think about architecture, now that they had found water.

"This is nothing," said Sriaugh dismissively. "Wait until we get to the Gompa Oasis, man. Now *that* is a fuckin' temple, let me tell you."

"Are we passing in that direction?" asked Gantsch, whose grasp of local geography was appalling.

"Yeah, dude," said Sriaugh with a chuckle, "I sure hope so! Unless we get seriously derailed, we are definitely following the old Imperial Highway to the Gompa Oasis, and southeast from there to Kiranesh."

"Oh," said Gantsch with detached acquiescence. "Great."

*   *   *

Back at the University, the two had done some studying together, but Gantsch had generally found it more efficient to study alone. He and Sriaugh were more commonly partners in mischief. The antics they dreamed up while drinking and smoking had brought them several severe reprimands from the university authorities. Gantsch still shuddered to think how nearly he had been expelled over that one incident... The incident had taught him an important lesson, though: *don't try to explain, just run.* This lesson had served him well just a short time later, during the administrative raid on the secret underground hiding spot. He still resented the memory of that raid; it had been so WRONG. The Den was just a place to go, to have a drink or a smoke, to socialize with scholastic companions or to get together with a female. Official interruptions were entirely uncalled for.

No matter. All that was a thing of the past. He was free now, freer than he had ever been, limited only by food and water supplies and the limits of his imagination. He and Sriaugh were nominally on their way home; but really they were just wandering, taking their time, free of responsibilities and worries and cares and concerns.

For this leg of their journey they were following the old Imperial Highway eastward from Varum to Kiranesh. Although the ancient road was now largely buried in drifting dunes, their plan was to follow its course, as it imperceptibly curved northeast from Varum to the Gompa Oasis, and then gradually back southeast from there to Aher Dahtl Dahl, in the foothills of the Rainbow Mountains along the East Coast of the peninsula. From that outpost they would thread the narrow pass through the mountains, and finally descend down to the modern port city of Kiranesh.

Of course, looking at a map, it would have been much shorter to head due east from Varum, avoiding the meandering of the highway; but it was impossible to pack enough water for a voyage straight across the hottest part of the Mohaani Peninsula. Without stopping at the various wells along the old Imperial Highway and, most importantly, the oasis midway through, the journey across the burning sands of the Zensai Desert would have proven deadly for them all.

As another alternative, it could have been far simpler to book passage on a boat at the port of Varum and sail the salt sea southward, around the point of the Mohaani Peninsula, then eastwards across the shallow southern gulf, and finally back up along the coast northwards to Kiranesh; but such sailing journeys were notoriously slow, and ridiculously expensive, and extraordinarily dull, except for the danger of being overtaken by pirates, who tended to take slaves and leave corpses; so all in all, the danger of dying of thirst in the middle of the desert was both more exciting and paradoxically safer. The simple fact that Gantsch did not at present have enough money to book passage on a ship determined the matter finally.

*   *   *

The first few days out, their interactions had been pretty minimal. When they set out from Varum, Sriaugh had been super tired, after those final few late-night parties; and for the most part, he slept, or lapsed into a trance state for long periods of time.

Meanwhile, Gantsch surveyed the breathtakingly beautiful rainbow rocks and stripes in the sand: colorful patterns within patterns which bent back over on themselves again and again, smaller waves inside of larger waves; patterns of infinite complexity stretching off for miles in every direction.

After a time, Sriaugh caught up on his sleep, and soon grew more conversational.

Over dinner that evening, Sriaugh grew positively chatty; erudite, even. "So many factors influence everything," Sriaugh was saying. "Anyone can make up explanations and rationalize them, but different explanations for the same event may be seemingly contradictory and yet both true. The universe is kind of complicated that way."

"I had a professor at the university who you would have loved," said Gantsch. "She was always demonstrating to us how the actual cause of every event that ever happened was more or less arbitrary; because there are always so many factors that influence any given outcome: so you can never trace them all."

"Really?" asked Sriaugh. "What sort of knowledge was this professor professing?"

"History," said Gantsch. "That was my main subject of study. I'm not sure I know why. Well, actually," Gantsch corrected himself, "I guess I do know why. It's because I'm interested in the subject. It's because by learning about history, I am able to tell you this story."

"What story?"

"This story. Listen."

Chapter 2: The History
of the Mohaani Peninsula

That evening, after their repast, as they leaned back, watched the stars, picked at the stuff caught between their teeth, and passed a bottle back and forth, Gantsch the History student told Sriaugh his traveling companion the lengthy tale of the land through which they traveled.

Sriaugh already knew much of the story; but with enough liquor in his belly, he no longer cared, and allowed Gantsch to talk at length about whatever he wanted to talk about.

"Though tough, arid, and inhospitable," Gantsch was saying, "the Zensai Desert has been inhabited by a variety of life forms since before time immemorial, longer ago than anybody can remember: ages and dynasties ago, long before the Fire Wars.

"In forgotten days," Gantsch continued, "long before the Empire, all the land from the tip of the Mohaani peninsula north to the entire southern part of the Nawathian subcontinent was covered with lush vegetation. In many places, there were vast sprawling forests along river basins, tangled jungles of spectacularly beautiful, mind-bogglingly huge trees. These forests were the splendid homes to an abundance of various life forms, who dwelt there and led a carefree existence among the trees with all their fruits and the wide variety of tasty organisms who coexisted in the forest.

"The local native peoples of the Mohaani Peninsula believed that there were gods in the water, gods in the air, and gods in the trees.

"The tree gods were especially important to the natives: not only because they were always surrounded by trees, but because they had discovered that the trees were made of smooth, easily sculpted material, which was surprisingly durable and weather-resistant. The wood also possessed the valuable property of burning with a sweet-smelling smoke, if heated to a high enough temperature. The locals all agreed that the wood was ideal for cooking their food and heating their residences.

"Yes, the locals touted the virtues of the forest, and the wood of the trees, and what a good life it was to live there; and slowly, word got around.

"All of which was a pity, for it had been such a nice place.

"Soon, more and more people started to trickle and stream in from the outside, all wanting a piece of their own. Some of these new arrivals went so far as to declare that the whole thing should be their own, on account of all the tremendous wealth and status symbols and deadly weapons they had brought along with them.

"At about this time, someone had the brilliant idea that you could build big boats with all these big trees.

"This was about the time that the Empire finally subjugated the native peoples of the Mohaani. The reader can easily imagine the result: lumber exports galore, with none of the proceeds going to the locals. The locals grew so poor that they were forced to burn down the remaining forests, and to then labor away their lives producing agricultural products for export. In a few short years, they either cut down or burned every damn last one of the trees.

"Then those new sunny spots got dry, surprisingly fast.

"Various agricultural and technological practices sped up natural processes, and all the topsoil blew into the ocean;

and the dunes marched over the face of the countryside; and this process was already pretty far along, when the Fire Wars ended the reign of the Empire and caused a major ecological and cultural disaster- a turning point, in a sense, for after that, things could only get better.

"The Imperial seat of the Mohaani region was once located in this part of the country, but it was all destroyed in the Fire Wars. Whatever hadn't been pulverized then was now either buried under huge dunes or sandblasted into its component molecules.

"In modern times," Gantsch concluded, "the entire Mohaani Peninsula is covered by the Zensai Desert, and all is barren, but for a narrow strip of irrigated agricultural lands near the coast, in the rain shadow of the Rainbow Mountains."

Gantsch's lengthy explanation trailed off.

"So, Gantsch, tell me," prompted Sriaugh after a pause. "What do you think? Did you learn a lot of interesting, useful information, in your pursuit of... of..." (he smirked at the possibility of saying a slang word for female genitalia at this point in his sentence) "of *history*, at the university?"

Gantsch took a swig, enjoyed the sensation as the liquor sloshed its chemical warmth through his body, and passed the bottle back. "Probably about the very last thing you could describe my studies as would be useful. Superfluous would probably be a bit more accurate. Interesting, yes, but not really helpful, in any strict definition of the word. Most of what I studied focused on the recent history of the region, you know, since the Fire Wars, because most of the old records were destroyed at about that point..."

"Wait a minute," Sriaugh challenged. "Did you just say," he paused, and started again. "Did I just hear you say that the Fire Wars are *recent*?"

"Well, yeah, comparatively recent, you know, in historical terms," agreed Gantsch. "The Fire Wars delineate the beginning of the modern era. It's all relative. Societies had been living here for probably tens of thousands of years before the Fire Wars, but our knowledge of the ancients is very limited: most formal records were destroyed, poof, all gone, and you can never really rely on on traditions and oral histories for accurate scholarly information- or at least that's what stuffy serious scholars say. In fact there's been this trend in the modern era of scholarship, and especially in Varum: all these people devote their lives to philosophizing, arguing, and writing dissertations which prove that you can *never* really understand history, because actually being there and experiencing something biases you, and your memory is fallible, but if you weren't there then you have to rely on someone else's account, and that is likely to be even more fallible. It's a tough call. After a while I decided I didn't really care nearly as much as my teachers and classmates all seemed to. It's important to learn from the past, but people still tend to make the same mistakes, over and over, repeatedly...

"But the problem with academia, is that all these historians want to propose general theories of history." Gantsch started speaking in funny voices. "History repeats itself, history is cyclical," a different funny voice for each new concept, "history *doesn't* repeat itself, it is linear; historical events are shaped by the personalities of a few influential individuals, the individuals who rise to prominence at any one time are riding a wave of historical inevitability; history contains observable patterns, the observable patterns in history are all projected onto our understanding of the past by scholars with too much free time... Personally I think that they're all right, sometimes, in some ways; and they're all wrong, in some ways, too. History does repeat itself, sometimes, sort of, but not really. Similar initial conditions do not always have similar outcomes, and besides, you never get exactly the same initial conditions twice; and if it's basically impossible to have identical initial conditions, then how can we ever know for sure?" He paused for a breath. "To tell you the truth I think it's all pretty random and unpredictable. Do we have any of that intoxicating liquor left?"

"The Askinthowa sect has a creation myth," mused Sriaugh, handing the bottle over to Gantsch and then leaning back to gaze upwards at the starry sky, "which ascribes the origin of the universe as we know it to a cosmic accident. The children of the gods, it is said, were playing around with some of their parents' more powerful magic potions unsupervised. The resulting explosion pulverized the world of the gods. The planets and moons are the cooled-off debris from the explosion, the sun and the stars are the embers which continue to glow."

"Yeah, I remember that one," agreed Gantsch. "Apparently, the unabridged version of the Askinthowa creation myth takes up six fat volumes on the High Priest's shelf on Dristra 4 in the Grundiq system."

Sriaugh laughed. "Yeah," he said, "that's right. But I think the moral of the story is reassuring, though," concluded Sriaugh wistfully. "It really tells us, 'You are not alone! There are sentient beings throughout creation who firmly, devoutly believe that someone must have made a mistake.'"

Gantsch laughed heartily. "That's for sure," he said. "So," he asked after a pause, "do you think we'll run into any wandering nomads out here in the desert?"

"It's certainly possible," Sriaugh said. "For a vast empty space, the Mohaani Desert is practically teeming with wandering bands of Dimpai: tribes of nomadic herders who wander the Zensai Desert along semi-seasonal migration routes. They sometimes trade with the settled cultures at the far extreme edges of the desert; but nobody sees them for most of the year, and they like it better that way.

"They wear flowing garments," he went on to describe the nomads, while Gantsch's attention wandered, "appropriately dyed to blend in with the somewhat freakish lands near the Rainbow Mountains; and they travel with herds of vebuthas, which are these hairy hardy edible domesticated animals with three dull eyes and very wrinkly besnouted faces."

"Dude," said Gantsch, slightly irritated at his companion's condescending suggestion that he might not know what a vebutha looks like, "I could totally go for a nice juicy vebutha sausage right about now, roasted on a stick over the fire."

"Yeah," Sriaugh agreed, "or a sandwich of thinly sliced and seasoned vebutha meat, inside a warm bread pocket, with crisp fresh vegetables and savory sauce."

"Damn, that sounds good."

Chapter 3: An Emergency
in the Wilderness

The morning after their stay at the ancient ruins, a renewed supply of water and sleep had revived their spirits. Sriaugh fed the six-legged dromi, and hitched the giant lizard to his dromi-cart while Gantsch packed up their gear.

Dromis were the preferred pack animal for long distance voyages through vast expanses of desert, due to their extraordinary strength and the hardiness which allowed them to work in direct sunlight for days without water. Adult dromis grow to at least twenty Imperial meters in length. They support themselves on sand with webbed pads of tough bony material; dromis have been documented to walk uninjured on sand at temperatures exceeding $150°$. Despite its appearance and smell, the dromi was nonetheless quite a gentle creature. Even so, many dromi-keepers have learned to their chagrin that one must always be wary of them, and watch out for their huge feet; for dromis are really rather stupid, and don't always look out for smaller creatures who might get in the way. Many fear them for this reason, although all such accidents, even the fatal ones, are due to operator error. Many others dislike dromis because of their ungainly appearance: for dromis have evolved to withstand the powerful blasts of windblown sand on the open desert; and thus their hide, especially on their faces, is gnarled, pocked, and always looks an unhealthy color. The chemicals in dromi hide allow the creatures to withstand the harsh sun of the desert for inordinately long periods of time without drinking any water, a veritable life-saver for any creature which spends long periods of time in the open desert. However, these same life-preserving chemicals give off a peculiar odor which is exceedingly harsh and unpleasant to the olfactory senses of most other Extarusian life forms. By far the most common complaint concerning dromis, always put forth by those who have been recently introduced to deep desert travel, is their scent, which is said to come off on anything that comes into contact with them.

If you have been riding a dromi in heat it is wise to avoid the presence of any dromis of the opposite sex for at least twenty-four hours.

*   *   *

Once the gear and their beast of burden were all set, the two traveling companions lightheartedly joked and told stories as their cart rocked and bumped along the road as it traversed the dusty miles to the distant rocky outcropping they had selected as a good spot for their midday heat break.

They totally failed to notice that the dromi was turning a greener shade of black, and that it was not scurrying at quite its normal rapid clip.

Instead, they continued their conversation from the evening before about the strange foreign customs of the Dimpai tribes.

"I hear the tribes are matriarchal," said Gantsch.

"I heard that too," said Sriaugh. "And their chiefs don't take husbands."

"No?" asked Gantsch, filing this factoid away in his social historian's brain.

"No," confirmed Sriaugh with a straight face. "The tribal women only mate with a male once, and then they kill him and eat him, just like certain kinds of insects."

"Really?" asked Gantsch, who was too drunk to care whether Sriaugh was bullshitting him or not.

"Oh, sure," said Sriaugh.

*   *   *

"When are we gonna get there Gantsch, I'm hot and I don't feel too well," said Sriaugh sometime later. He had already made several similar utterances, and Gantsch was beginning to be forced to admit to himself that he felt ill as well. In fact the sensations arising from his abdomen made him imagine the sharp rods he had seen used as roasting sticks; he felt as though he was being pierced by one, its point glowing red from being over a fire for longer than was strictly necessary.

They were sitting inside the cart, taking shelter from the sun, Dworon, which was approaching its daily zenith. It would soon be time for them to find a shady spot to spend the hot hours of the midday. Gantsch looked at the tall outcropping they had selected as a good spot. It had seemed like a reasonable goal, when he'd seen it earlier; but it did not seem to be getting any nearer: it merely shimmered and wavered with the distant heat.

"I don't know," Gantsch confessed. Sriaugh was the one with experience driving a dromi cart; he himself had no idea where they were going, or how long it might take to get there. "But I don't think we're going as fast as we have been," he noticed of a sudden. "Do you see that big outcropping up there, sort of on top of a rise? I thought it looked shady but... echugh," he coughed, and sniffed. "It doesn't seem to be getting any closer."

"What's wrong?" Sriaugh moaned, emotionally weaving a frantic, jangling fiber into the texture of his voice.

"I don't know. Maybe the dromi feels sick too. Maybe he feels sick for the same reason you do."

"But their biology is so different! Surely we wouldn't get sick from the same thing that makes a dromi sick, would we?"

*   *   *

The bacterium multiplied. They ate cell walls. They gobbled up nerve fibers. They erupted capillaries.

Gantsch and Sriaugh's immune systems recovered from the initial shock of the attack and began to fight the infection, slowly but surely.

Their dromi's immune system was more susceptible to this strain of microorganism.

The dromis of centuries gone by were the bacterium's principle carrier. The beasts had left their dung near the well, and some of the fecal bacteria had seeped into the water the next time it rained. Rain was more frequent back in those days. The bacterium had lived in that particular well ever since, and the water's lethal effect on dromis who drank from it gave rise to a Dimpai legend about a peevish demon who inhabited the well. As time passed and the well began to dry up, the hardy little microorganisms went into a state of stasis: they hibernated, lay dormant, and mutated just a little bit. Even so, most of the little spirochetes had died from lack of food source, until finally these thirsty travelers made the mistake of drinking out of the wrong well. By now the bugs were pissed off and hungry. They blazed up the giant hexapedal lizard's neural pathways, straight to the dromi's central nervous system, the energy source... and

ATE HOLES IN ITS BRAIN

Gantsch and Sriaugh felt more nauseous with each jolt of the cart. Gantsch racked his memory for details but was unable to prove to himself that the cart had jolted this much yesterday. He didn't consider that the real difference was his perception. Whereas yesterday he had been sitting on top of the cart, his attention diverted by the scenery and light conversation, at the moment he was taking shelter from direct sunlight inside, sensitized to the minutest bump and aware of little else.

Suddenly the cart stopped its forward motion. It stayed motionless for a few minutes, during which time its occupants neither moved nor spoke. Finally Sriaugh said, "Gantsch, why-"

But at just that moment the cart turned on its side. Gantsch and Sriaugh found themselves on the wall, near the ceiling, underneath a heavy, uncomfortable, shifting mound of chests, packages, furniture and provisions which represented all their possessions in the world.

Gantsch was pinned underneath a heavy piece of furniture which for some reason Sriaugh had insisted on bringing along. Gantsch attempted to free himself, but the only reward he earned for his struggle was a searing pain in his leg.

Sriaugh was luckier, for although he was bruised by a box full of Gantsch's books, he landed on the box and not vice versa. Some fresh fruit fell and squished on his head, but caused him no injury. He found he was able to open the cart door; standing on the book box, he hoisted himself out.

"Hey!" cried Gantsch in pain; but Sriaugh did not respond. Seeming dazed, his movements uncoordinated, Sriaugh made no sign that he had heard his friend, as he awkwardly climbed out of the overturned wagon and disappeared from view, leaving Gantsch terrified, alone, trapped, and in pain.

Chapter 4: The Wanderers

Quithtar emerged from her tent groggily. Walking to a large rock nearby, she checked the solar collectors she had set up the previous evening. Since sunrise, the reflectors had been focusing bright Dworon's incredible fusion power on a water jug. The reflectors had done their work well: her jug was burning hot to the touch. She opened its stopper, and poured a generous handful of fine-ground roasted qafay seeds into the hot water.

Quithtar reckoned the solar reflectors had been a good trade for the small bronze statue of a sandstorm goddess. Quithtar had been fond of the statuette, a delicate piece of Kiraneshan artisanship. She still remembered the crowded colorful marketplace where she had haggled with the smiling dark-skinned stall owner to purchase it. She would have to get another, the next time her tribe returned to the East Coast.

For now, she was leading her tribe in the opposite direction. The Smyrna were a loose association of four or five family groups. They were returning with their vebutha herds from a recent visit to the underground city of Scruggs, north of the Rainbow Mountains.

The Rainbow Mountains, like all the rocks of the Zensai Desert and the surrounding regions, are composed of colorful composites of minerals. The desert sand itself is purple, or green, or red, or stripes and swirls of these and other colors. The rock formations, in the rocky parts of the desert, are all streaked with various bright colors. Eroded by the seasonal rains and the yearlong windblown sands into bizarre shapes, the desert scenery includes tall thin spires, inverted pyramids, arches, domes, sometimes rocks which resemble a face or an Extarusian life form. It is by observing these optical delights that travelers amuse themselves during the long hot days while traversing the long slow stretches of straight road.

From the far southernmost tip of the Mohaani Peninsula, the Rainbow Mountain Range runs northward all along the eastern seaboard, and spans the entire peninsula in the north, all the way to the narrow neck that separates the peninsula from the Nawathian mainland. On the other side of the neck, North of the Rainbow Mountains, the Nawathian mainland has been consumed by the fearful "al-hassud xinpau," or "sands of death," a desert so vast that few expeditions have survived on it for long.

After leaving the underground city of Scruggs, Quithtar's tribe had followed a coastal route across the mountainous narrow neck that joined the broad Mohaani Peninsula to the vast mainland of Nawathia. Their course, southwards overland from the foothills of the Rainbow Mountains, intersected with the old Imperial Highway, and from there followed its well-established direct route to the Gompa Oasis.

Everyone in the tribe looked forward to visiting the Gompa Oasis. The oasis was the most reliable water source in flattest, most arid desert of the whole Mohaani Peninsula. It was rarely abandoned; various nomadic peoples came there from many miles around to replenish their water supplies. A festival atmosphere often predominated there. She was looking forward to it.

Quithtar's companion man emerged from the tent, yawning and stretching. Dimpai chiefs did not take husbands, as it tended to make the men arrogant; but this particular man had been Quithtar's companion for many years, and was the father of her children. He smiled at her with sleepy eyes and went behind the tent to take a piss. Returning, he kissed her on the cheek, and she handed him a steaming mug full of delicious bitter hot qafay. They were joined a few minutes later by her eldest daughter, beautiful Balhudailadishtarya, who emerged like a blooming desert cactus flower from a smaller tent nearby.

Quithtar quaffed the qafay in large gulps in between tasks, as she and al-Bert took down their tent, packed it into a pack, and strapped all the gear and water jugs to Ride with well-worn leather straps. Their daughter Tarya worked nearby, efficiently packing up her own tent.

"I see your gross smelly digestive bladders are all hanging out in the breeze this morning," Quithtar remarked casually to the beast of burden as she buckled and tightened the straps. "There must be a healthy crop of rintsyan plant growing nearby. That," she mused, as she prepared to mount Ride, "has got to be one incredibly hardy plant, to thrive in this part of the desert."

Soon the camp was lively with the bustle of morning, as the adult nomads prepared for the day's journey and young children ran here and there, chasing each other and squabbling over the choicest pieces of dried fruit.

After breakfasting and making ready, Quithtar climbed up onto Ride's back, situated herself in the saddle, grasped the reins, and pointed the dromi's head in the direction the tribe would travel until the sun got too high in the sky. Ride began to traverse the sand in her characteristic odd six-legged scurrying motion.

Quithtar observed the ritual phortawanay pipe sacrifice to the Sandstorm Gods, imploring them to grant the group safe passage.

Then she handed the pipe to al-Bert.

He was a good companion man, she thought, watching al-Bert as he sat in prayer beside her. He was still a relatively fit and attractive man, even as they grew older together; a good father to their daughter, a ready hand with the vebutha herding, trustworthy with the market money; and when they made love, he almost always brought her to orgasm. He was a bit moody at times, but never violent. She had experience with a number of other men, and on balance, she was far happier with al-Bert than she had ever been with anyone else.

"It almost sounds like the author is setting me up to decide that I'm unhappy with my companion man," Quithtar thought to herself. "But the reader who thinks so, is going to be very disappointed."

"We give praise to the gods of the desert," al-Bert said, and raised the pipe to his forehead in a ritualistic gesture. "Bless this caravan," he intoned, "bless this journey with good fortune. Take us to our destination, bring us success, and protect us from untrustworthy strangers, and protect us from the Sandstorm Gods."

"The Sandstorm Gods," Quithtar echoed happily, as she felt the sweet phortawanay euphoria begin to kick in.

Quithtar wasn't really sure she believed in the Sandstorm Gods, but she believed in deadly sandstorms, and she rather enjoyed the phortawanay pipe sacrifice ceremony, so she figured if there were some sort of invisible beings controlling the weather out here, it was just as well to be on good terms with them.

*   *   *

Like many of the Dimpai, Quithtar rode her dromi bareback. Enduring the beast's malignant odor was thought to strengthen spiritual fortitude and physical stamina and endurance. City-dwellers might complain about dromis and try to avoid them; but desert nomads have no such choice. No other pack animals were capable of making such a long journey through the waterless wilderness; and without a pack animal, it would not be possible to bring a herd of vebuthas across the wasteland.

Through the years, Quithtar had grown so accustomed to the dromi's rancid smell that she needed no carriage, but sat directly on Ride's back, amidst an extensive collection of jugs, bundles, and baskets of miscellaneous stuff that constituted all her personal property in the entire Universe.

Quithtar and her people followed no roads, frequenting high places where they scampered over rocks and the wind picturesquely blew their hair.

The wind picturesquely blew the hair from Quithtar's sunburned face.

Quithtar had traveled this route many times, but the wise traveler never allowed herself to feel comfortable in such an environment; she must always be on her guard: for the pass was dangerous, the mountains treacherous, and the weather unpredictable. The possibility of avalanche was the most glamorous fear, but the weather was the greatest danger, for the sandstorms of the region had a 100% mortality rate for travelers caught in them.

Quithtar looked ahead. The scene was indescribably incredible- the mountains, their cliffs, crags, crevices, crevasses, canyons- and she was almost all the way to the top. She was enjoying the full splendor of one of those natural focal points of the Withinwithout; she was at the center of a mind-bogglingly vast expanse of incredibly intricate landscape, the shapes and colors of the geography infinitely varying, infinitely subtle, worked on such a huge scale... She reflected that not even a large dose of the powerful Omasu she had brought back from the pale-skinned cave-dwellers in the north could produce splendors on such a grand scale.

"Ach, Ride," Quithtar said softly to her dromi, "when the wind blows, I wish I had thick eyelashes like yours, to keep the dust out of my eyes."

The wind was blowing Quithtar's hair quite picturesquely, and her descent into the foothills of the Rainbow Mountains involved a number of dramatic scenery changes, but she was too pestered and perturbed to enjoy it. She couldn't remember doing anything that would offend any of the Dimpai gods, yet the pestilence which plagued her today certainly seemed like divine vengeance.

Quithtar felt the tickling sensation as another one landed on her leg. She let it sit there just long enough to start feeling safe; then she crushed it with a sudden smack, shaking its slimy innards from her hand onto the desert sands. She cursed in some foreign tongue. She didn't know what these things were, but she did know they were really ruining her morning. They were just a little bigger than her smallest digit and they could fly. Flicking them off was useless because they just came back, and if she tried to ignore them they always bit her eventually. At least they didn't seem to inject any poison, she thought, looking on the bright side. They almost seemed to be simply nibbling on her out of curiousity; but that thought did not make the sensation of their mandibles entering her flesh any more pleasant.

Quithtar eventually remembered some half-comprehended tales she had heard of travelers harassed by swarming things called Buking Fiters. At the time, she had not really believed the stories about the cumulative effect of the swarms, stories about small animals and unattended children picked clean to the bones. She shook her head, again, hoping she didn't have any in her hair. She didn't need this. This whole being-someone-else's-lunch thing just totally offended her sensibilities. Quithtar decided in favor of an early and extended lunch break.

"We deserve it," she explained to al-Bert. "First we got up early, and hit the road, and then we crossed some pretty rough terrain there, and then we got chewed on by those..." and she proceeded to colorfully describe the hungry Buking Fiters.

Some hours later, Quithtar picked a rocky outcropping off by itself as a likely site for shade and a picturesque place to chill for a couple hours. She was pleased to find, on reaching it, that a road ran by it. Although the Dimpai needed no roads, still this particular road was a useful landmark.

"Hey, Ride you see that?" Quithtar asked the dromi. "Yeah, you see it," she answered for the mute creature, "I bet you can smell it too. There been thousands of dromis over that one spot of land; but they ain't here now. This is the old Imperial Highway, Ride! We're making good progress. Good girl, yeah."

Sitting beside her, al-Bert smiled silently at her friendly chatter.

*　　　*　　　*

Many Sihvees, not knowing any better, have spread the urban legend that dromis eat invisible plants. Actually this statement is misleadingly simplistic, for the rintsyan plant is merely very well camouflaged. To get around this little complication, dromis evolved specialized eyes which see in the ultraviolet light spectrum. When they find choice specimens of their favorite vegetation, known to the local scientific community as *dromifodder invisibus*, the six-legged giants slobber, and let smelly digestive bladders hang out from seemingly unnecessary orifices on their undersides, all of which is recognized by those who lived around dromis as just part of the package.

Quithtar could lend no assistance to the process of the dromi's subsistence, so she left Ride alone to forage for herself. Behind her, al-Bert was preparing a midday meal for the children; he seemed to have things more or less under control. Quithtar concentrated instead on her climb up the irregular rock, to a narrow ledge from where she could see the day's route. This climb required no little amount of contortions, exertions, clambering and scrambling. Thus when she finally reached a comfortable cranny which would provide her with some shade, she was determined to enjoy the moment to its fullest. She seated herself upon a ledge overlooking the vast plain, savoring more than would have been strictly necessary for expediency's sake the splendor of the place itself, and those little luxuries with which she entertained herself while there: her little lunch, her little tea, her little smoke.

Quithtar had been sitting up on the rock apart from the tribe, enjoying her solitude and these divine worldly pleasures for some time, when Gantsch and Sriaugh passed beneath her on the old road. The two Sihvee youths were completely unaware of her presence, for her immobile posture and elevation above eye level protected her from being noticed by them, and indeed her trancelike state nearly shut out her notice of them; although they were so foreign that their manner of dress caught her attention. Even at a distance, their severe, restrictive clothing instantly identified Gantsch and Sriaugh as members of the conformist coastal Sihvee society.

Quithtar's attention had wandered and she was prepared to ignore the Sihvees, until some words of their conversation drifted up to her where she sat, and caught her attention. It was just a seemingly nonsensical and meaningless fragment of conversation in a foreign tongue, although as it happened to be the official tongue of a land where she had done some trading barely half a year ago, the literal meaning of the words hung in her mind unbidden for some time after the words were uttered.

"I don't know much about them, you know," the distant, strained voice of an unseen stranger with a Sihvee accent was carried up to her by the wind and the unpredictable acoustics of the rocks from down below. "It could be anything, it could be little maggots eating his brains for all I know."

Hmmm, Quithtar thought to herself. *That's a curious conversation... I wonder if these fools made the mistake of stopping at the Demon Well?*

Quithtar looked down the road towards the travelers who had just passed him. The dromi pulling their cart looked ill, limp, drooping, somewhat too slow, somehow the wrong color. Her curiosity aroused, Quithtar watched the little company's progress, trying to convince herself that it was only natural that they should seem to be moving slowly: it was just a trick of the perspective, because she was elevated far above them, watching them traverse a vast area; and besides, the poor dromi was encumbered with a cart. City people. They were always too proud to get a little dirty. The foolish Sihvees had probably brought with them all their largest, heaviest household goods. Quithtar wondered if they were provided against highway robbery. She had no intention of taking up that particular line of livelihood, but she made passing acquaintance with all types in her journeys, and she was well aware that she had met many nomads who would not scruple to appropriate the goods of travelers who were so obviously inexperienced.

Suddenly she realized that the dromi pulling the cart was weaving, almost staggering. After mentally abusing the ignorant way city dwellers treated pack animals on long distance journeys, she scrambled and slipped down the steep slope.

Ride had curled up in a shady spot to digest her rintsyan lunch and nap; she looked up in surprise as Quithtar approached.

"Sorry to disturb your nap, old girl," Quithtar said reassuringly. "Bloody world can't take care of itself."

But Ride was not favorably disposed to this proposed interruption of her repose and bared her teeth. Though dromis are generally gentle, friendly creatures, they are quite massive and capable of asserting their own will; when crossed, they never lose a disagreement.

Just as Quithtar was contemplating this issue, Ride stopped suddenly and lowered her head, making Quithtar's center of gravity shift uncomfortably forward. After flailing briefly, she regained her balance and peered down the neck of her six-legged mount. Ride was sniffing a large mound of greenish brown globules which had clearly come from the digestive bladders of a large lizard quite recently.

"It looks unhealthy," Quithtar's daughter Tarya observed.

"It sure does," Quithtar agreed.

"Disgusting," summed up al-Bert, holding his nose.

Bright-shining Dworon had nearly reached the horizon by the time Quithtar arrived on the scene. The dromi, still tied to the cart, had died in a particularly grotesque position, and helpless Sriaugh was sitting next to it with his head in his hands. At first, Quithtar thought the dazed Sihvee was bleeding profusely from a traumatic head injury, but on closer examination she realized there were chunks of exotic fruit smeared all over the young man's head.

"Look, fresh fruit," Quithtar said to her companion man, and pointed at the mess. "Do you see?"

"He must have come from Varum only recently," al-Bert agreed.

They dismounted and walked towards the dazed young man leaning against his overturned cart. He stared up at them with wild, uncomprehending eyes.

"What happened to your dromi?" asked Quithtar, but the young man made no answer. "Are you injured?" Quithtar persisted, but the Sihvee did not seem to understand. "We can help you," Quithtar offered. "Are you traveling alone?" But the young man seemed to be in the grip of an illness, perhaps the same brain fever that had killed his dromi.

Still trapped beneath heavy furniture within the overturned cart, Gantsch was uncertain at first if he was actually hearing someone speaking to Sriaugh outside, or if he was merely hallucinating in his delirium. Finally he called out, "In here, I'm in here." His voice didn't work very well at first, but after several repetitions of his requests for help, Quithtar's feet descended through the door.

Chapter 5: The Tribeswoman

I can't see. I don't know what it is I can't see. My head feels like its been wrapped up in blankets, my ears feel like they're full of boiling water

Pain

Cough cough cough cough spit phlegm cough cough cough break for air cough cough cough cough cough *can't breathe* gasp vomit cough cough cough cough cough spit cough sob

Lay still don't move If I don't move it doesn't hurt as bad

*　　　*　　　*

"We'll just let him sleep for a while," said Tarya's mother Quithtar, gently wiping the vomit from the fair face of the strange Sihvee youth.

"Poor dear, he just needs to rest," said the medicine woman. "At least he's coming out of it now. He'll be okay."

"That's good to hear," sighed Tarya, genuinely relieved.

So the three of them left the strangers to sleep.

*　　　*　　　*

Balhudailadishtarya of the Smyrna people used to play on a flutelike instrument to entertain herself. She loved to go off by herself to find canyons, to listen to the sound of her vlayolasth bounce between the rocks. She also played while in transit; and for her nomadic people, "in transit" was a lifestyle and a tradition. She had been in transit ever since she was born. Although they almost never left the Mohaani Peninsula, her people made a practice of frequently changing residences, often at short notice.

So she played her vlayolasth. She was a big fan of old songs and could play by memory a number of traditional tunes, although lately as she had been playing a lot she had been writing some new songs of her own. When she was particularly pleased with the direction one of her improvisations was taking she would sometimes do a little dance in time, always moving forwards but rotating in her path, a little dance she had always loved doing, swaying her lithe body with the music.

Tarya (her full name was too cumbersome for daily use) was teaching herself to play music in accordance with the transcendentalist music theory of Rheild.

There was once a mystic, philosopher, prophet, and traveling musician named Rheild: the official founder of the Smyrna religion, and the author of their only sacred text. Rheild lived in the days just a generation or two before the Fire Wars. Some say that she claimed to be the reincarnation of the Great Prophet Gaizuth, who had lived several thousand years previously. Regardless of whether or not this is true, she gave people a lot of good advice for free, and reinterpreted the ancient religions in terms of a positivist, pacifist, ecological philosophical view.

Rheild had proposed that music was not only a form of meditation but a direct line of communication to the Old Gods. None of the Smyrna really took the Old Gods all that seriously anymore, but they kept them around because it was nice to have a sense of tradition. Besides, the religious ceremonies invoking all the Old Gods involved the ingestion of a psychoactive spice, the Holy Omasu, a tradition with which nobody really wanted to do away.

*   *   *

Gantsch and Sriaugh awakened to find themselves in a strange tent, camped on a broad sandy plateau. Someone had left them fresh rich qafay in earthenware mugs set on a stone nearby.

Bewildered, still sick, but eager to analyze new data, the two recent graduates sat at their campsite, drinking their qafay and watching the Dimpai go about their morning business, watching the Dimpai women bend over their cooking pots, watching the Dimpai men, who were watching them back with a mix of curiousity and mistrust.

After a time all the tribesfolk gathered together for some sort of communal religious ceremony, singing in an ancient language, unaware that the song they sang had never made literal sense, even in the language of its composition.

Gantsch and Sriaugh sat apart, feeling strangely isolated even in the midst of all the social activity of these people who had saved their lives. Trying not to openly stare, the two young men continued to contemplate the Dimpai women in their nomad clothes. Finally Sriaugh said, "We're going to have to go meet them."

"My thoughts exactly," said Gantsch. "Got a good plan for the introduction?"

Sriaugh felt his pockets, patted one a few times and said, "Yeah." He would say no more until he and Gantsch had walked across the plateau and fully into the circle of the Dimpai camp.

There was some confusion during the initial introductions. Gantsch misunderstood the word, "chief," and didn't realize that the chief of the tribe was standing in front of him. It never occurred to him that the chief might be a woman. He did not even look directly at her, at first, not wanting to offend the Dimpai by paying too much attention to someone else's squaw. Instead, he immediately glanced at the men standing off to the side, trying to figure out which of them was the chief he was supposed to greet.

"Here," said al-Bert somewhat impatiently, and pointed at the austere woman standing calmly in front of the two young men.

"Oh, I, uh, sorry," said Gantsch, embarrassed. "Hi."

"It's an honor to meet you," said Sriaugh, who was handling this situation much more professionally.

"Truly an honor," echoed Gantsch, feeling extremely foolish. "Thank you for, uh, for having us. I mean, for curing us. And, uh, for meeting with us."

Quithtar graciously ignored the gaffe.

"Hey," Sriaugh said to the circle of nomads, "Do you guys got any Omasu?"

Stony faces. They were not about to volunteer information about their most valuable commodity.

"I'll trade you good phortawanay for it."

Slight expression changes.

"You want a sample?"

Still no words, but a smile or exchange of glances here and there.

Sriaugh filled a pipe from a leather pouch. With a pair of tongs he picked up a hot ember from the cooking fire. "I sacrifice to the Sandstorm gods for peace and longevity," he said. He dropped the ember on the bowl, puffed and passed it around the circle of nomads in their loose desert clothing. He refilled the bowl several times.

The tribal elders said nothing at first, but the one nearest Sriaugh silently nodded his head to nobody in particular. Then he leaned over and said something to another elder, who looked pleased. After a quick show of handsigns, the elders convened an impromptu meeting with their guests and presently agreed to a barter arrangement: *Kindank* phortawanay from the floodplains south of Varum in the West, in exchange for the highest quality Omasu from the Foreign Trading Post in the underground city of Scruggs, carved out of the living rock deep in the north face of the Rainbow Mountains.

*   *   *

Sriaugh was still too sick to travel, so the Smyrna had generously offered to remain camped there until he was well enough to move. Although he was recovering more rapidly than his friend, Gantsch himself also still felt a little weak and queasy, so he was glad for the rest. Traveling across the desert was surprisingly draining, even though the dromi did all the work.

The Smyrna had a game with which they occupied most of their free time. It was said to have religious overtones, but it was mostly a game of coordination and fast reaction times which involved keeping control of a ball in the air by touching it only with certain parts of the body. Gantsch attempted to participate, but the tribe members who had grown up doing it were all infinitely better than he, who had never tried before.

Lost in his meditations, Gantsch borrowed a ball intended for this game, and went off behind a large rock at the edge of a shallow ravine behind the camp to practice in privacy. He kicked the ball, dropped it, kicked it again, chased it. After a while he had exhausted himself physically, but he kept kicking the little ball, kick, pursue, toss, kick, miss, toss, kick, pursue... He began to feel that there were an infinite variety of wrong moves in this game.

Suddenly he had the uncanny feeling that he was being watched. Startled, he whirled around, prepared to defensively hurl the ball at his unknown audience. Frustrated, embarrassed at his lack of skill, and more than just a little paranoid, he would not have reacted well to anyone watching his flounderings.

Then he noticed she was female.

Then he noticed she was female again.

She was a nomad, clearly; and Zumwatsu only knows how long she had been there. She was smiling, she was laughing at him, although she stopped laughing when she saw his facial expression.

"I know, I'm not very good at it," he said, beginning to feel embarrassed and sheepish. He tried not to stare too blankly at the most beautiful feminine figure he had ever seen.

"But you're learning fast," she said. "You're getting the idea, doing really well for a Sihvee." Her accent was thick, so thick as to almost be its own dialect, but by random chance or divine intervention it was basically the same language that he spoke.

Gantsch was ready to change the subject. He didn't want to dwell on his lack of skill in his conversation with this inexplicable phenomenon who had appeared at the edge of his ravine, an odd musical instrument in her hand. "What are you doing here? Who are you?" he said, then cursed himself for saying such things, as her presence was far more logical in this locale than his own.

"I came to play my vlayolasth," she replied. "My name is Balhudailadishtarya."

A shiver went up his spine.

"Your name is *what*?"

"Balhudailadishtarya," she said with a smile and a slightly different inflection.

Gantsch paused for a second, considering if he should say what he wanted to say. He said it.

"Will you say that again please?"

"Yes but then you have to tell me your name!" she laughed. "My name is Balhudailadishtarya, but most people just call me Tarya. It's shorter, you know, easier to call out over long distances when they are trying to tell me that they are going to pack up camp and I had better come along if I don't want to get left behind."

"What?" he said in bewilderment. His brain seemed stuck, unable to process her words.

"I said, what is your name, Sihvee boy?" she demanded with a laugh.

Gantsch had never heard this expression applied to himself before, although he was vaguely aware that "Sihvee" was a somewhat derogatory Dimpai term for city dwellers.

"Oh. I'm Gantsch."

"Gantsch," she said with a certain surprise, as though she had been expecting a taste of sugar and found herself with a mouthful of salt. After a moment she added, "Is that the whole thing?"

"Well," he said, feeling embarrassed, "my full name is Gantschronymous Arindicus; but I usually go by just Gantsch, because it's, uh, shorter," he trailed off.

The beautiful exotic young woman nodded sagely. "May you see many beautiful sunrises, Gantsch," she said sweetly, feeling perhaps she had been too hard on him. "How are you enjoying your stay with us?"

"It's good," he said, feeling at a loss for words. "I mean, I'm sure grateful to you all. You have no idea how frightening it was, when I was out in the middle of nowhere, traveling on the ancient highway, over there, somewhere, you know, when the dromi died, and Sriaugh and I got sick. When you friendly passerby brought us here, you saved our lives." He had to crane his neck upwards and shade his eyes a little bit to look at her up on the top of the ravine. "What is that thing?" he asked, pointing to the elongated, slightly conical tube in her hand, with little holes in different places and colorful pendants hanging off it.

"What, this?" replied Tarya. "Have you never seen a vlayolasth?" And, as he had hoped she might, she jumped over the edge and skittered down the sand to stand next to him.

"It takes big breathing to make sound," she said. Taking a lungful, she produced a tender melody with a melancholy edge and a delightful rhythm. They were both instantly caught up in the music, and she had played several very soulful phrases before she grew suddenly self-conscious and broke off in mid-phrase.

They could both feel the tension in the air, a semi-sexual sort of hormonal static electricity, the fragile thread of an unwound cocoon which, had it been overtly mentioned, would have instantly broken, transformed into something common, dull, unglisterous and gross.

Gantsch tried to smile encouragingly but the expression on his face was more sort of bewildered. "That sounded beautiful."

Tarya was genuinely pleased. "I'm glad you think so. I like the way the sound bounces off the rocks in places like this, that's why I came out here. I'm always on the lookout for places like this with bouncy acoustics; when I saw that we were going to set up camp near that big flat rock you don't even understand how stoked I was."

Gantsch shifted his weight and stuck the game-ball in a pocket. Then in a flash of inspiration he pulled it back out and said, "What are these things called again?"

Tarya laughed. She had a good laugh. Gantsch wanted to hear her laugh again.

"It's a hekwaixak," she said.

"A what?"

She laughed again. Gantsch could not help but smile.

"A hekwaixak," she said again, slowly.

Gantsch made a few pitiful attempts to pronounce the word, then was suddenly hit by a powerful pang of discomfort-around-a-desirable-member-of-the-opposite-sex. "Well, I uh I guess I had better leave you to your music," he said, stumbling on his words.

She smiled a smile that outshone the sun. "It was very nice to meet you, Gantsch."

"No, really, Tarya, the pleasure was all mine."

*   *   *

Some time after lunch, Gantsch found himself seated upon a high sunny rock in a remote place, when a distant movement caught his attention. He did a double-take, and had trouble finding whatever it was. At first he suspected it was merely a heat shimmer but then it came back into view. It was a large ornaweg, flying along the ridge of the next rock outcropping, its huge membranous wings soaring on the wind. From what he had learned of the local landmarks, he was struck by the singular wonder that he could see the ornaweg at all, so far away over the expanses of desert. This must be a truly immense specimen.

Gantsch's mind wandered with the bird. Sometimes, as columns of air shifted in the heat, refracting and distorting beams of light, the ornaweg would disappear entirely; and then, because it didn't want to feel lonely, Gantsch's mind would disappear too.

Thus overwhelmed with food, phortawanay and deep thoughts, Gantsch's mind shut down entirely, without warning. His eyes closed, his head sagged, his breathing slowed, he snored.

Awakening in the late afternoon, Gantsch realized what a poor napping place he had chosen. He had been fully exposed to the sun the whole time he was asleep, and could now look forward to two weeks of painful, peeling skin.

Clambering down the hillside, his mind was so caught up in his recent error that he committed another. Failing to notice signs that he should have recognized, Gantsch cut his hand on a rintsyan plant, of the variety known to the scientific world as *dromifodder invisibus*. How those dromi creatures could eat the damn things he never knew, for as far as he could tell the plant's outer layer was all armor and spikes. Gantsch's experience so far had been that whenever he came into contact with a rintsyan plant, it drew his blood. Infuriated, he aimed a perhaps poorly-considered sharp kick at the plant, only to miss, perhaps due to second thoughts mid-swing, and instead kick the rough red rock out of which the prickly plant grew.

Disturbed by this outrage, a squat roly-poly leathery round thing with hallucinatorily huge eyes and a face like a steamrollered mummy blumbered and fanoozled out from behind a nearby rock and began greggering at him. Gantsch didn't like the tone it took, in fact he didn't appreciate its greggering at all, and he was about to kick the little beast even harder than he had kicked the plant, when he recalled that when angered the badjhaag could be vicious and bloody; and besides, his toe hurt.

Gantsch walked back to the Smyrna camp, carefully watching his feet the whole way.

At least I saw the badjhaag on the surface, he thought when he passed a thin spot in the ground which he very easily could have fallen through if he had not been looking for it. The badjhaag's presence meant the presence of a thin spot over a burrow, and few travelers who fell into such burrows live to tell the tale.

Gantsch recalled from University the strange story of a surprised scholar who had survived a somewhat stupid fall into a badjhaag burrow. The scholar's name was Gwaberthicus Kwapithicus of Pruawll. After first falling into a badjhaag burrow and then slowly recovering from his many painful injuries, Gwaberthicus Kwapithicus had written an account of his experience, a copy of which is preserved by the Kathingakathka Society in Balsac.

"Descending from rocks on which I had payed my respects to Zumwatsu and broken my fast," wrote Gwaberthicus, "I fell through the ground and met with sharp teeth. A burrow of vicious creatures, surprised by my accidental intrusion into their sedate lives, nearly deprived me of my own precious life. I was too busy trying to get out of the hole to get a good look at them at the time, but I have since had opportunity to examine a deceased specimen at length.

"Badjhaags are bizarre burrowing beasts. Their round leathery bodies are about twice the size of my head, with a very strange-looking contraption at one end, presumably a combined eating and respirating mechanism. This knobby, twisted, very hard device underneath huge eyes was the part of the beasts with the sharp teeth. I thank almighty

Zumwatsu who certainly aided me, for I am certain that without his divine assistance the little buggers would have pulled me apart.

"The large, complex eyes of the badjhaag," Gwaberthicus went on in his rather lengthy description, accompanied by a pretty decent hand-drawn sketch, "can see in both the glaring radiation of the desert sunlight, and in the total darkness of their underground burrows, via the infrared spectrum. Badjhaags eat a variety of vegetation which is related to *dromifodder invisibus,* although somewhat more prickly. As vegetarians, badjhaags are generally harmless and uninterested in the other mobile life forms with whom they share the desert; but they have evolved fearsome teeth, to allow them to eat the prickly plants: and when frightened they can be vicious. There are many reported cases of travelers accidentally falling through the sand into badjhaag burrows, but few accounts of survivors."

And Gantsch wanted to LIVE! There was so much to live FOR! Great scenery, the good-natured companionship of his slow-witted dromi, the thrill of making a trade, the thrill of the hunt, the thrill of seduction.

There were worse things to step on, too. Whereas the burrowing Badjhaags will gang up on you if you fall through their roof, a gargantuan gargathod will get so pissed off if you step on it that it will eat you in one bite; which is a problem, because it's difficult to avoid stepping on a 700-pound burrowing creature that lives just below the surface and has a bony shell the color of sand and the texture of rock: because you can't see the damn thing...

*   *   *

Approaching the outskirts of the camp, Gantsch stood alone in a clearing between the spindly dry plants and the prickly plants.

"Balhudailadishtarya," he said aloud.

He took three steps forward, and paused.

"Balhudailadishtarya," he said again, this time with a different vocal inflection.

He shifted his head from side to side; brought an upper appendage to his chin; and furrowed his brow deeply in thought.

"Bal hu dai la dish TARYA?" he speculated quizzically, as though each syllable were its own statement in a ponderous argumentative philosophical discourse.

"BAL HU DAI LA DISH TARYA!" he exclaimed triumphantly.

Enter Sriaugh.

"Gantsch, what the hell are you gabbling about?" he asked.

Without thinking about his response, Gantsch blurted out the beautiful name once more: "Balhudailadishtarya."

Sriaugh examined his companion's eyes. "Have you been raiding my stash?" he accused humorously.

"No," Gantsch protested, and turned to face him, and then turned back away. "I," he said, and faced Sriaugh again. "Uh," he said, and turned away once more. "I'm trying to nail the pronunciation of a Dimpai word," he concluded with some embarrassment.

"Oh, yeah?" chuckled Sriaugh. "What does it mean?"

After a pause, "I think it means, Divine Perfection," Gantsch gushed.

*   *   *

"You seemed surprised," said Tarya later that evening. "The first time you met our chief."

"Oh, yeah, I guess I was a bit confused," Gantsch admitted. "It's just," he explained self-consciously, "where I come from, a 'chief' is a man. It's like, what the word means."

"Well, then what do you call a woman who is a chief?"

"I don't know," Gantsch confessed sheepishly. "It's never come up. A chieftainess, I guess? There aren't any. It just doesn't happen."

"How peculiar," said Tarya. "Well, out here, our chief is a woman, and that's how we use the word, 'chief.'"

"That's great," said Gantsch hastily, stumbling over his words and unable to complete a coherent sentence. "I have no problem with it, you know, I just had never heard of it, I didn't, uh, I didn't know there were Dimpai chiefs who are female."

"All our chiefs are female."

"All of them?"

"Of course! Didn't they teach you anything at that University of yours?"

"Well, yeah, they taught us a lot, but not that."

"If they didn't teach you something that fundamental, then what in the world have you been studying all this time?"

"Oh, lots of stuff! Mathematics, and history; astrophysics, and chemistry; biology, foreign languages, and a solid grounding in Zumwatsunian theology; and at least three different kinds of high art: are all required for graduation. I liked the history classes best," Gantsch concluded, "but it was all very informative."

"And yet, you know nothing of the cultures of your neighbors, the people who live next to you, right here on our own Mohaani Peninsula."

"Well," he admitted, "there's so much to learn about, that it's impossible to know everything about everything; so instead, we learn a framework, with a solid grounding in the hard sciences, and then from there, using that as a starting point, we're encouraged to go out into the world and, you know, learn *more* about everything. We know there is much we don't know. It would be foolish to think you could learn everything there is to know in just a few short years. The more you learn, the more you realize there is to know."

"That's all fine," she objected, "but this 'foundation' of yours, the basis for all of your other learning about the whole entire world, it omits entire cultures, your own neighbors! I think that's a pretty huge gap in your foundation!"

"I'm not going to argue with you," said Gantsch patiently. "I wish I knew more. Honestly," he went on after a brief moment's reflection, while the other set about straightening out some camp implements, "sometimes I wonder if the framework we're provided is at least partially designed to benefit the stability of our own social system, and to what extent that would tend to limit our thinking. But that's got to depend," he mused, "on what area of study one chooses to pursue..."

"Well, we *used* to let the men run things, sometimes," she explained, "but they were always finding reasons to fight with the other tribes. There was always something. They were so quarrelsome, there was never any peace. Now we have a rule that men can lead the army but they can't decide when to use it."

"Whereas," mused Gantsch, "the city of Varum, where I attended University: under its puritanical King Szathzia, the place stresses Conformity and really unimportant sorts of things: very strict laws, extremely hierarchical society, and the patriarchal priesthood preaching the rigid doctrine of Almighty Zumwatsu..."

"It sounds like a nightmare," observed Tarya.

"Well anyhow," said Gantsch, "thank you ever so much for rescuing us. We literally would have died if your tribe had not found us. I don't even know what happened, but my gods, I was so sick!"

"It's because you stopped in an accursed place. Our people never go near those particular ruins," she chided him.

"No, never?" he asked, somewhat surprised. "I don't see why not. It seemed like a nice place, all things considered. I mean, it's all rather falling apart, but there are still some statues there which are really quite tastefully done, and high walls which could often provide shade, and a well which never goes dry..."

"Be that as it may," she said sternly, "the Dimpai refuse to avail themselves of any pleasantries the place might afford; for we say that the well in that place is inhabited by a demon."

"Is it," he said doubtfully.

"It is," she replied sagely. "You yourself were nearly consumed by the demon's fire."

"Huh," he said. "So what you're saying is, the well is poisoned."

"I suppose that's one way of putting it," she answered loftily.

"Well, we didn't know that," said Gantsch sheepishly. "It would be nice if there was a warning of some sort," he pouted. "You know, somebody could put up a sign or something, saying, 'Danger, Poison, Don't drink the water,' or something, you know?"

"Let the traveler be wary," she said, quoting a popular proverb. "Who would put up such a sign? There is no one to put up warning signs: no government here, no community, nothing, no one. There is just a vast emptiness as far as anyone can see. The various Dimpai tribes who roam this desert are independent bands. We don't look out for one another, and we often compete with one another for scarce resources. We're independent. We're adults! There is none to watch out for us here: none but the cruel gods, who play capricious games with our very lives, as if we were nothing more than expendable game pieces."

"So you just let travelers drink the poisoned water and die if they don't know any better," he summarized.

She shrugged. "Yes."

*   *   *

"Well, listen," said Chief Quithtar later, her long hair blowing in the wind as she gazed off into the dry desert distance. "Now that you're both up and about, it's time we moved on. We wouldn't normally have stayed in this place for more than one night, but we didn't want to make you travel when you were so sick."

"Well, we thank you deeply," said Gantsch. "You have most certainly saved our lives."

"It's very kind of you to help us get better," agreed Sriaugh.

"And I know there's no way we can ever repay you," continued Gantsch, "but if there's anything we can ever do for you, of course, please just let us know."

"It is the traveler's code," replied Chief Quithtar seriously. "All we ask in return, is that you pass it on. If you ever see someone in need, you provide them help, no matter who they are."

"We will," promised Gantsch and Sriaugh most gravely.

There was a slight pause, so Gantsch instantly began babbling mindlessly to fill the uncomfortable silence. "And we just want to let you know," he said ingratiatingly, "that we have really enjoyed spending time with you, and learning from you. You have a fascinating culture, and some amazing, uh, people." He grew suddenly embarrassed as he suspected everyone around him was well aware which specific person he was particularly fascinated with; and he was entirely correct.

"It seems to me that the people like you, too," Quithtar said with a friendly twinkle, "and since it seems you are headed in the same direction, at least for the time being, you are more than welcome to travel with us to the Gompa Oasis."

"Thanks!" said Gantsch enthusiastically, and only then looked to Sriaugh to see if he agreed; which he did.

"That would great!" agreed Sriaugh. "Only," suddenly he hesitated, and sighed. "I know my dromi died of dysentery or something, but I really don't want to leave my carriage behind."

"Is there, like, maybe a dromi that you could sell-" began Gantsch, filling in the blanks for his friend.

"How much more of that phortawanay do you have?" interrupted Chief Quithtar.

"Well," Sriaugh speculated, "back in the carriage, there's uh..." Then in a low, flat tone, he named a surprisingly large number.

"I wasn't aware you had that much," laughed Gantsch with a certain new respect for his friend.

"It's just business," explained Sriaugh defensively. "And I can get more," he told Chief Quithtar hurriedly. "Back in Varum. I have a good connection."

"We won't be headed back that way anytime soon," said Quithtar, "but if we ever get out in that direction, we'll be sure to look you up."

"So, where are you headed after the Oasis, then?" asked Gantsch as casually as he could. He would have liked to travel with the lovely Balhudailadishtarya all the way to Kiranesh; so the Chief's next words came as something of a disappointment to him.

"When we leave the Gompa Oasis," she said, "we'll continue our journey south, until we reach the distant outpost at Kramwek; and from there, we'll probably follow the coast towards Varum; and from there we'll head back north again, towards Scruggs, on the far side of the Rainbow Mountains."

"Scruggs," recalled Gantsch. "Isn't that the underground city at the southern edge of the al-Hassud Xinpau, in Nawathia? You've been there?"

Quithtar nodded. "The people of Scruggs are miners and survivors: a hardy folk, and a touch cruel. They have little contact with the outside world. They feel they have little need for outsiders, for they grow their own food in hydroponic tanks, and they mine their metals, and they mine their fuel-stones, and they generally try to avoid foreigners; but they do enjoy the occasional delicacy, and as such they will trade valuable ores and precious stones for fresh vebutha meat. Also, they are one of the few sources we have for the Holy Omasu, which they make from a fungus that grows in their dark underground caverns."

"You have a reliable connection for Omasu?" asked Sriaugh with an awestruck gasp.

"Yes," said Quithtar, "if we have something they will trade for it. They tend to charge a hefty price in vebuthas; but in exchange for about one-fourth of that huge stash of phortawanay you keep flashing, I believe they will trade us a shitload of Omasu. So," she concluded, "that is our asking price. We will sell you a dromi, in exchange for one-fourth of your phortawanay."

"Thank you," said Sriaugh after a slight pause where he ran some mental calculations, registered surprise, ran some calculations again, and determined that the Dimpai chief was being very generous. It was an excellent exchange rate. In point of fact, the Dimpai were practically giving the dromi away for free. The transportation beast was far more valuable than the supply of dried herbs Quithtar had asked in trade. Here, stranded out in the middle of nowhere, the two Sihvee boys had no real bargaining power. If they'd wished, the Dimpai could have demanded the Sihvees hand over everything they had, in exchange for a priceless dromi; and faced with the alternative of dying stranded in the desert, the two students would have had no choice but to accept. The terms Quithtar had named were friend prices, to put it mildly; and both the young men were well aware of the generosity of the offer.

"Thanks very much," echoed Gantsch; for although it wasn't his carriage, and it hadn't been his dromi that had died, and it wouldn't be his dromi that was being purchased, and it wasn't his phortawanay involved in the exchange: still, he felt that he was a beneficiary of the arrangement. Even so, there was still something more on his mind. "You have done so much for us already," he said, "but if I may ask..." Everyone was looking at him, which made him nervous; but Gantsch kept talking nonetheless. He asked to go back for his books and personal items that had been left behind in the overturned dromi cart. The cart itself would have to be abandoned, he suspected; but there were a few items that he didn't want to lose; especially some of his precious books.

"We'll backtrack down the road to the scene of your accident," offered kind Quithtar. "It's only a few miles away. When we find it, some of our men will help you fix the carriage, if it turns out to require fixing."

"If we're lucky, it just needs to be detached from a dead dromi," quipped Gantsch, and instantly regretted it. He should have shown more respect for the unfortunate beast of burden, especially in a moment when his hosts were showing such generousity. Sriaugh scowled in displeasure, but Quithtar and the other gathered tribespeople politely ignored Gantsch's gaffe.

*   *   *

At this time of year, the band of nomads traveled by day. Their pace was unhurried but constant.

The nomads brought with them enough fuel to build camp fires for several days, but whenever possible they did not even unpack these stores. Instead, they built their evening fire from such dry grasses, weeds, and reeds as might be found nearby. Of course, these were scant, and burned quickly; so the nomads were always on the lookout for occasional weatherworn logs, and any twisted branches jutting from the sand. These pieces of sand-softened grey wood were all that were left of the great forests which had once covered the Mohaani Peninsula. Occasionally, they would even find bits of what might have once been old houses and garden gates, in the days before the Fire Wars, now nothing more than disintegrating bits of charred and unrecognizable lumber, buried in the sand.

The evening camp fires were not primarily used as cooking fires; but rather for warmth and enjoyment. Much of their food was dried fruit, nuts, and such vegetables as could store reasonably well in the heat; so it didn't even need to be cooked. When they cooked meat, they used burners manufactured in the cities and fueled with rendered fat or distilled al-quhaal.

"Wow," said Gantsch, "this food is great. In Kiranesh, where I'm from, the people eat salty, fatty, highly processed foods of poor nutrition. The food is mass-produced in factories, using some of the few technologies that remain from before the Fire Wars; and it is prepared in bulk for maximum efficiency. It is tasteless and lacking in nutrition, so that the people are sickly and fat but always still hungry and kind of depressed."

"No wonder you're always such a barrel of laughs," said Sriaugh.

*   *   *

Gantsch had been practicing hekwaixak by himself in the evenings and early mornings on a very regular basis recently. He was trying to improve his skills; but proper execution of the moves was more difficult than it looked. The hekwaixak always flew off in a frustratingly wrong direction.

One day, a couple campsites after his initial encounter with Balhudailadishtarya, Gantsch was down in another ravine, challenging himself with the foreign hekwaixak again, when she came around a bend.

Gantsch felt very self-conscious attempting to play his newfound sport around her, but as he stopped she smiled and motioned for him to continue.

Tarya watched him as she approached. She liked the way he looked; he was kind of cute, in a thin and studious kind of way that was offset by the weatherbeaten ruggedness imposed on him by their travels. He moved awkwardly; she found his unfamiliarity with the hekwaixak inexplicably humorous. When she was standing near enough, she tried to explain that for the Smyrna the game had metaphysical connotations. "Try to think of the motion of the ball as the flowing of energy through the cosmos," she said in a lilting chant with a voice like warm honey. "By concentrating on it, you can control that energy, and guide that motion, fluidly, all the way from one point of contact to the next."

Distracted, Gantsch missed particularly badly. The little ball demonstrated the effects of gravity, and discovered its affinity for the ground.

"Often there is no time to think about it consciously," she sympathized. "The conscious mind is too slow. By thinking about one's actions for too long, many an opportunity may be missed. The hekwaixak teaches the art of reacting. Try to watch it only at the apex of its trajectory. Feel its motion. Let your understanding of movement relax; move with the ball, not against it. It's a gentle touch. Try to keep it low. Gentleness is key." She snuffled humorously. "You learn a lot about the shape of your feet, too."

Her words were confusing him, making him feel flustered; and the awareness that she was watching him bumble suddenly became too much. He tossed the ball to himself and kicked it to her.

She caught the hekwaixak on one foot and stalled it. Then she began kicking it to herself, back and forth, working up speed until she was dancing where she stood, her appendages flying in all directions around her, the ball circling her the way an electron cloud circles the nucleus of an atom. Then she tried to smile at him. It broke her concentration and the hekwaixak flew off at an odd angle. She laughed, shrugged, and continued to smile at him.

Gantsch boggled.

"All Smyrna begin hekwaixak training when young," she explained. "It is an integral part of our religious education. Rheild did not invent the game, but we are told that she was a supreme master at it, and that she endorsed it as a guide to the cosmic interface of enlightenment."

"What?" Gantsch reflected that there were many things about the world for which his education had left him entirely unprepared.

Tarya tossed the ball to him. Being deep in thought his reaction was far too delayed. He looked at her and noticed that she was looking at him quizzically.

She was thinking that there was much she wanted to teach this Sihvee, perhaps even much she would like to experience with him. She said nothing.

"Let's start with this one," said Gantsch finally. "Who is this lady, Rheild? I keep hearing about her these days, from you guys; but I had never heard of her until my encounter with your people, a few days ago. Back home, everyone is into ancestor cults, and they get paranoid about sorcery and witchcraft all the time. The only god they talk about a whole lot is the Almighty Zumwatsu. No Rheild."

"No Rheild?"

"No Rheild."

"There is much to tell you."

They bantered the hekwaixak back and forth in silence a little longer.

"I think this is easier with two people," Gantsch said after a time.

"It is," she agreed. "We complete a circuit."

They made eye contact. Gantsch had been out in the hot desert sun for a long time, and Tarya was extraordinarily beautiful. This game of footbagging was not the only circuit he wanted to complete with her.

Chapter 6: The Mystic

"Our ancestors," said Tarya as she deftly slung the footbag back and forth between the various angles of her appendages, "believed that Dworon, the sun, was the chief of all the gods; and that the moon Ktliven was his wife. They were busy, hard-working gods, and could only devote their full attention to Extarus for a few months of the year, which is why we have seasons. So every year, towards the end of summer, my ancestors would hold ceremonies where they would ask the gods to go attend to their business elsewhere, and allow the rains to come back, because it was getting too hot."

"That's a beautiful story," said Gantsch.

"Yes," Tarya agreed, "but our suns are really superhot fusion reactors, we know that."

"You know a lot, for a nomad," said Gantsch, intending his remark as a compliment, but instantly regretting it.

Tarya bristled. "Just because I live a nomadic lifestyle, doesn't mean I'm ignorant."

"I didn't mean-"

"Anyhow," she interrupted, and he was glad when she resumed her more conversational tone, "we still have the ceremony every year at the end of summer, but its significance has changed, now that it no longer rains on the peninsula."

"I would love to learn more," Gantsch encouraged her to keep talking, for he loved the sound of her voice, and her lilting Dimpai accent.

So Tarya told him about the philosophy of her people: its historical roots in pre-apocalyptic tradition, and its founder.

*   *   *

The Empire before the Fire Wars was the product of a rigid social hierarchy, supported by a religious system that aid out a strict code governing the behavior, and the share of the division of labor, that was assigned to each socioeconomic class. The state religion taught the people, "Work is your salvation." Religious observation, sacrifice, and prayers were required several times a day; and that was just for the merest hope of a possibility of being happy in the next life: the one they believed would follow death. There was no chance for improving one's lot in life, here on Extarus. Obviously, those at the top of this hierarchy benefited considerably from this system, especially since they got to eat the sacrifices...

"Work will make you happy," the system taught the people.

There was a girl from this society, who one day whispered to her friend, "But what if I'm not happy with *this* work? What if I think I might prefer some *other* kind of work?"

"Oh, don't say that," said her friend, looking around to ascertain that none had overheard. "You mustn't ever say that."

The girl who had asked the question was named Rheild. Following the advice of her peers, Rheild kept her thoughts to herself for many years as she grew up. She went along with the prescribed behavior, and professed to believe in the prescribed ideology: but always, she observed; and always, she questioned what she observed.

Then one day, a time came when Rheild, now a woman grown, felt she could keep silent no longer. She began to travel the land, encouraging the people to do their own thing.

"Hey, no, wait, you guys have got it all wrong," Rheild preached to the people. "Don't do what you're doing. Don't work so hard and stress out all the time and fight wars. Just chill. Seriously, just chill out, man. That's Enlightenment, right there: when you can just chill. Stop worrying about some imaginary afterlife. That's not important. What's important is what's right here, right now. The best things that can happen to you, are going happen in this lifetime, in this world, right here, right now; so focus your mental energies on making more good things occur."

Naturally, the heads of state at the time were not happy about this new doctrine, when they heard about it. The system regards free thinkers as dangerous; and although some of her followers helped her to hide out for a while, it was not too long before the Empire martyred Rheild.

But the Imperial forces were too late. Rheild had openly encouraged people to do what, deep in their hearts, they had been wanting to do their whole lives. Although following or spreading her teachings was declared treasonous by the Empire, this did not stop Rheildism from becoming a major social movement.

In the generations before Rheild began preaching, the Empire had made organized attempts to suppress the native religion, and to replace it with a militarily enforced faith of its own: an Imperial faith, which declared that only the governors of the Empire could function as intermediaries between the common people and the gods. The natives, encouraged by Rheildism, rejected this philosophy in exchange for Rheild's, which was based on the fundamental concepts of the grandparent religion, but which was updated and interlaced with many of the metaphysical, political, spiritual, and theoretical ideas of Rheild herself. Her teachings spread throughout the land.

Enraged, the government executed a lot of religious leaders, calling them insurrectionists, rebels, traitors, terrorists, anarchists; accusing them of treason. Her followers pointed out that Rheild had not advocated violence, and that furthermore her teachings were in direct continuity with the religion of their grandparents. Finding themselves accused on the basis of their beliefs, her followers started practicing mass civil disobedience. The Empire ramped up its crackdowns.

Seeing this internal conflict and recognizing it as a weakness, a hostile foreign power stoked the social divisions, and talked up the discontent to weaken the very fabric of the Empire's society. Encouraged by subtle propaganda, the people accused each other of perpetrating improbable conspiracies. People called each other names in cyber chat rooms, and got into street brawls in real life.

After decades of such civil strife, the Empire was weakened, and eventually unable to withstand a military assault by its foreign rival. The foreign rival launched a triumphant invasion, with assaults from the air, ground, and sea. Desperate, the Emperor ordered the use of the weapons of last resort. The foreign power retaliated in kind.

The entire world was engulfed in flame. Most of the people died. Most of the learning and most of the technology were lost.

The cities and arable farmland of the Mohaani Peninsula and the neighboring subcontinent of Nawathia were both reduced to desolate deserts, dry and nearly lifeless: the Zensai Desert, which covered most of the Mohaani Peninsula; and the al-hassud xinpau, or "sands of death," which covered the entire southern portion of the Nawathian mainland.

Thus the power of the Empire was annihilated, along with all its technology, in the Fire Wars; but the basic tenets of Rheildism survived, along with a few folks who had the good fortune to already be way far out in the desert, a long ways away from anything else, when the Fire Wars started.

* * *

"I've heard the history of the Fire Wars before," said Gantsch, when Tarya had concluded this insightful dissertation. "We studied it in school. But it's amazing to me that my classes didn't cover the role of Rheildism in the runup to the conflict. It seems to have been super important."

"We say," Balhudailadishtarya told the Sihvee boy, "that you city-dwellers have inherited the culture of the Empire. Perhaps you were not taught about Rheild for the simple reason that your rulers still do not want you to know."

"Oh, that couldn't be!" Gantsch protested. "My university prizes learning above all else!"

* * *

"The religion of Rheild's ancestors used to almost stigmatize the overuse of the mind," Balhudailadishtarya was telling Gantsch later that evening. "They feared an interruption of the Cosmic order, so they pointed at the lifestyles of all the other animals and said, 'Look, we must be more like them; that is how the gods wish us to be.'"

She let this thought sink in for a moment. Gantsch's mind wandered off with it.

"That's not such a bad thing," he suggested philosophically. "After all, the Fire Wars themselves were the outcome of thinking too much."

"I suppose you could look at it that way," she said, but that wasn't the way she preferred to look at it, so she decided to be argumentative. "Thinking too much about enmities and grievances brought about the violence and destruction; but thinking about the consequences is certainly not what led to those bad decisions."

"The consequences," Gantsch said, and nodded. "Right."

"Anyway, Rheild didn't agree with that; because obviously a great deal of thought went into her philosophy." Tarya looked over at Gantsch, suddenly self-conscious. "Do you mind that I am telling you so much about Rheild?"

"No, not at all," he assured her. "Please tell me more, I'm fascinated."

*   *   *

Rheild's philosophy analyzed many old myths of the traditional gods from a new perspective. This made her ideas easily accessible to the general public, thus aiding in the growth and tremendous popularity of her philosophy. However, she made a decisive break with tradition, by proposing that all the gods were subordinate to an all-pervading energy field. Any and all action by anyone or anything derived its energy from this energy field, a Force which Rheild dubbed the Withinwithout. She proposed that, upon dying, a being's spirit-energy rejoined the greater Withinwithout, an undifferentiated boundless whirling mass of energy. One would be undifferentiated, that is, unless one had been trained in the meditative arts, which Rheild discussed at length. Rheild proposed a way to maintain consciousness and to direct the energy of one's spirit after death through training in this world.

Death and what happened afterward formed only a minor fragment of Rheild's extensive teachings. She was far more concerned with the potential for the properly trained mind to shape and redirect the flow of energy in this world. Rheild philosophized about the innate energy of all objects, and described sound as another form of energy. Her philosophy thus advocated an understanding of music. Rheild encouraged her followers to practice all forms of art, from the visual arts to the martial arts; but she believed music to be one of the highest forms, a complex refocusing of the Withinwithout which was perceptible to the terrestrial senses yet could bridge the consciousness gap to an interface with the cosmic. It is said that Rheild was a master musician, and when not meditating spent much of her time practicing one of the various instruments she played.

It is also said that Rheild was a master of the traditional art/sport/martial art/physically active transcendental meditation known as hekwaixak. Rheild believed that hekwaixak was a sublime combination of all other art forms, and she promoted it as the most advanced method of understanding, knowing, being, working within and redirecting the forces of the universe, jiving through the cosmic interface between the tangible which can be tanged by the senses and the subtangible energy field that makes it all tick.

*   *   *

The ancient forest tribes had traditional religious ceremonies in which they drank a bitter beverage brewed from Omasu as a way of inviting the Old Gods to come play with them, down here on the surface of the terrestrial world. These ceremonies had been popular throughout the centuries, because if you drank enough Omasu, the gods always came. The traditional religion prescribed Omasu ceremonies and other meditative invocations of the gods on many different occasions: solstices, equinoxes, birthdays, weddings, funerals, comet sightings, eclipses, and particularly sunny days. The Empire outlawed these festivities, along with everything else about the native religion, for invoking deities with the wrong names. The Empire was however ultimately unsuccessful in their attempts to suppress the ceremonies themselves. During the years of the Empire, illicit spirituality was conducted only under the strictest of secrecy, for discovery meant death.

Rheild was in attendance at one such surreptitious event one summer solstice. She climbed to the top of a high rock and sat there, surveying the landscape, feeling in harmony with and of supreme importance to the cosmos.

She was speculating about the meaning of it all when she suddenly witnessed the destruction of a chunk of space debris. Battered, smashed, and sandblasted by its long travel through deep space, disabled long ago by an encounter with a particularly large asteroid, an interstellar probe, launched hundreds of thousands of light years away by a civilization which had almost surely destroyed itself by this time, was yanked from its course by the star Dworon, pulled into the gravitational field of its fourth planet, and as the young prophet-to-be watched in starry-eyed wonder, it burned up in the nighttime sky of Extarus, leaving a huge streak, a bright trail of flames across the darkening evening sky. Due to the power of suggestion, many of his subsequent hallucinations were shooting stars of one form or another, as well.

Rheild was convinced that she had been sent a message from the gods. She believed it was a sign that the time had come for her to hold her silence no longer; and indeed, that very night she began expounding her philosophies to any who would listen, although on that particular first night there were many other participants who all wanted to expound on their own theories. It took some time and explanations before people started to realize the true import of Rheild's philosophy.

In the end, Rheild concluded, "So we're intelligent. Oh, well. That's kinda good, and kinda bad. Sometimes intelligent beings have these crazy ideas. Occasionally these crazy ideas have disastrous consequences. Sometimes our crazy ideas are self-destructive, or just plain stupid. By considering our actions, we can try to avoid doing misguided things, ourselves; but we cannot expect to prevent misguided actions in others. Instead, we should try to recognize stupidity and evil when we see it; and we should try to enjoy our lives to the fullest: because our intelligence increases our appreciation."

In later days, Rheild herself implemented provisos for impromptu Omasu celebrations, which she called Unforeseen Holy Days.

*   *   *

"Over time," Tarya was telling the Sihvee scholar, "Rheildist philosophy de-emphasized the Old Gods and started seeing them as symbolic. 'There is a Force,' they preached, 'which is extant in the Universe, flowing through everything: a binding energy field. When you die, your spirit energy rejoins with this Force, undifferentiated: unless you know.' For whether you believe that sort of thing or not, Rheild has proposed a way to maintain consciousness and direct the energy of your spirit after death through training in this world.

"Most modern Rheildists claim that Rheild herself didn't really believe in all the Old Gods at all; they say she just used them in her parables to illustrate points, as a sort of metaphor. Others (those who can chill a bit) recognize that maybe she did believe in them, but that it's not important, because you can accept her philosophy without bringing gods into it at all.

"You see, Rheild's philosophy deals with the relationship of the self to the world: including the self's relation to the self, to other individuals, to other life forms, to the ecosystems in which we live, to the planet we live on, to the other planets and suns and distant stars, and to the whole entire cosmos.

"When the Dimpai learned the pacifist philosophy of Rheild's teachings, they willingly accepted those pacific ideals as good policy, yet nonetheless retained their traditional practice of arming themselves and training for combat.

"The Dimpai religion advocates peace as the wise course of action, but the Dimpai people practice the art of war. There will always be conflict, not necessarily from the outside world; so it is necessary to be able to defend oneself."

"I could never kill somebody," said Gantsch in a waking dream-state if euphoria, overwhelmed by love and sun and phortawanay.

"Blanket statements such as that are dangerous," warned Balhudailadishtarya. "I never *want* to kill anyone; but unforeseeable situations arise. But there are some people who do want to kill: and they carry weapons, provoke fights, and look for opportunities to start trouble and instigate violence. I am not one of them. My people avoid society because there are so many of them."

Chapter 7: Traveling Together

It took more than half a moon cycle to reach the Gompa Oasis. Some of the Smyrna began to grumble. "We will proceed much faster when we have finally rid ourselves of our new Sihvee companions," one snarked snidely.

The grumblers were few, however, for Gantsch and Sriaugh had made friends with many of the nomads. Sriaugh's bold recklessness and boisterous, cunningly outgoing manner won the admiration of many; his jokes and stories showed the nomads that they shared a common element of the life-experience with city dwellers. Gantsch was quieter than his friend, but polite and attentive, and though more an observer than a participator in most social exchanges, his occasional witty remarks almost always provoked laughter.

Gantsch and Sriaugh found themselves participating in many nomadic group activities: playing hekwaixak; smoking kind phortawanay; looking after the three-eyed besnouted vebuthas; attending the engaging story-telling circles and even the unfamiliar religious ceremonies. There was much about the Smyrna way of life that they found admirable and even enjoyable.

Gantsch was even finding that the usually arduous task of sand-trudging was aided by the nighttime travel habits of their companions. This switch was increasingly important, for the days were getting progressively hotter, as the group headed ever deeper into the desert, and the season of high summer approached. Soon Gantsch could hardly believe they had ever attempted to travel during the daytime. He thought back to just a few days previously, when sitting in the wagons became unbearably uncomfortable in such intense heat. His whole body had felt like he was melting from the sweat in the sweltering sun; the air was almost too hot to breathe: not even the temperature tech, left over from the fallen civilization of the days before the Fire Wars - not even that could cool off a transport in direct sunlight on a day such as this.

"What were we thinking?" he asked Sriaugh, "traveling with the sun overhead? Bad idea! Hot! Hot!"

There was but one solution: to hide from the sun under a reflective tent, to sleep through the heat of the day, and to only travel during the night, after blazing Dworon sank below the horizon, and the air went from punishingly hot to merely warm and reasonably breathable.

The major drawback with night travel was, it became very difficult to see, once the great moon had set; so the tribe's objective, each night, was to travel as far as they could by moonlight, wearing out their dromis until the great moon Ktliven had set; and then to set up camp where they would rest, sleep through the day, and await the next evening. There were entire days when they only traveled a few miles, but it was a good life.

Enjoying the fascinating company of Balhudailadishtarya, Gantsch did not even notice the passage of the time. Normally a quiet sort of fellow, he was surprised at how much he had to say to her. She had much to tell him, as well; and now that they had started talking, their conversations would last throughout the travel and into the morning, after the sun had come up and everyone else was asleep.

"So, are you the only nomads in the desert?" Gantsch asked casually during one such free-roaming conversation.

"What?" she scoffed. "No! Are you being silly?"

He didn't answer.

"At any given time," Tarya explained more gently, "there are a variety of different tribes, bands and cooperative living arrangements, all out and about wandering: strolling, marching, frolicking, or trudging through the sands of the vast Zensai Desert."

She certainly has a way with words, Gantsch thought with admiration

"Some are members of one extremist religious sect or another. Some claim ties to some sect which had existed as desert-dwellers before the Fire Wars. Some are essentially pirate bands, preying on other nomads, wayfarers and small communities in outlying areas.

"The vast expanses of desert appear barren, dry and lifeless to those who don't know," Tarya told hims philosophically. "Many travelers make the long trek through the Zensai, cursing every step. Some fail to complete the crossing and die blaming the desert through parched lips. These travelers can't understand why the Dimpai would want to spend all their time under the hot sun. The Dimpai know that these travelers just don't understand. The desert actually has a surprising variety of life forms which have adapted themselves to survival in its harsh conditions. If you die out there, they are the ones who will eat your carcass. Most of them choose not to live in the vicinity of major thoroughfares. Indeed, with such a huge expanse of desert, totally full of places where they might choose to abide, most of the desert-dwelling life forms have chosen rather solitary lifestyles.

"Outsiders lump all the wanderers together under the title of Dimpai. The term Dimpai is not actually a word used by the nomads of the Zensai Desert to describe ourselves. It could more accurately be described as a word applied to any nomadic tribe by the city-dwellers who really don't give a toss about the individual identities of the tribes themselves. You see, we each identify by our tribe's name; so none of the tribes would ever refer to themselves as Dimpai except perhaps in jest."

"That's good to know…   However, as I understand it, the generalizations are not entirely one-sided, for the Dimpai refer to any and all town or city dwellers by a similarly distasteful generic term: Sihvees."

"Why?" she asked innocently. "Shouldn't we? I mean, you are all basically the same, right?"

"As it happens," said Gantsch, "we did briefly discuss the history of the Dimpai tribes in one of my History classes at the University."

"I feel confident," she told him, "that everything they taught you was wrong."

"I realize they didn't teach us about modern Dimpai culture," he said, "and I'm sure that seems like a tremendous failing; so I understand your cynicism: but I *did* extensively study the transformative historical era that may have led to the formation of your entire culture. You don't even want to hear what it was?"

"Sure, if you want to waste your time," she teased, then winked and licked his face like an animal.

"Okay," he said slowly and deliberately, as he wiped her saliva off his cheek. "There is a popular myth," he began, "that describes how all the different tribes now dwelling in and around the Zensai Desert are the descendants of the so-called Alhuquavins (a name which in the ancient Synskrete tongue means, 'the smelly ones who eat the sand') who left civilization before the Fire Wars as a protest of the evil of society, prophesying a judgment which many said had come to pass with the Fire Wars themselves. These believers, the legend continues, were ascetics, and intentionally inflicted torture upon themselves to expiate sins.

"After the Fire Wars, those who survived believed they had been 'saved' by one of the gods. Some declared utopic Paradises; others declared the reign of 'freedom,' in other words, lawlessness, and generally went crazy."

"I don't know how popular that myth can be," Tarya commented, "since I have never heard it."

"Well, it's popular enough that they taught it in my school," Gantsch said.

"Not sure that means much," Tarya scoffed.

"Well, it means something," he huffed defensively, "because, as often happens, it turns out that this legendary explanation is a vast oversimplification of historical facts."

"Is that so," she said, growing bored.

"Yes!" Gantsch continued enthusiastically. History was after all his favorite subject. "You see, the myth omits an important part of the picture; because before the Fire Wars, there were already a few tribes living in the remote Zensai Desert (which was much smaller, then). Some of the tribespeople were religious ascetics, just like the myth says; others were political or social extremists of one sort or another; some just liked the warm arid climate and a few around the edges with less migratory ambitions even practiced agriculture.

"But then," he continued the recitation, "after the Fire Wars scorched the planet, the dry winds blew the advancing sands. In a few short years, desert had consumed a considerable portion of the land mass, and it continued to gnaw at its borders as time passed.

"Having survived the Fire Wars, most of the central region's remaining population fled before the advancing sands, escaping south by boat across the seas in search of the Islands of Plenty. But at the same time, a small countercultural movement sprang up among many young people, who saw potential opportunities in a lifestyle change: you know, get out of town, get away from parents and former lovers and people you owe money to; be a desert dweller. There was something of a fad for a while. All the truly 'with it' people were proclaiming their distaste for civilization and society by dropping out and 'going mad,' i.e. joining a nomadic tribe, get it?"

Tarya looked at him blankly.

"Oh, well, uh, so apparently," Gantsch resumed his narrative self-consciously, "based on what we can deduce from the historical record, most of the whackos who 'went mad' subsequently cursed their fate for a while and then ran away back to the surviving cities on the coast; but a dedicated few decided that they actually really liked living the desert way: and they became the ancestors of the Dimpai."

"My ancestors," Tarya said with a hint of wonderment.

"Your people," Gantsch affirmed.

"I like you," she said suddenly.

"I like you too," he said in surprise.

"I want you to become one of my people," she went on.

Gantsch was surprised, and uncertain how he should react. "What does that entail?" he asked, before realizing what an honor she had offered him and how rude he was being with this response.

Tarya, affronted, did not answer.

*   *   *

Gantsch was awakened from an uneasy dream by a disharmonious droning sound. He shook his head to ascertain that he was not in fact still dreaming. The droning sound seemed to resemble some sort of religious invocation, many voices chanting tunelessly in some incomprehensible foreign language.

At just this moment a sharp and unpleasant bit of sand found its way into his eye and precluded all other observations for the time that it took his eye to work up sufficient moisture to flush out the intruding bit of pulverized rock. Now wide awake, he peered over the rocky ledge upon which he had gone to sleep with his traveling companion who was now nowhere to be seen. He boggled at the sight below.

The droning sound was in fact coming from a band of singers, all singing totally and painfully out of tune from one another.

Trekking through the middle of the desert as they were, not close to anything resembling a watering hole, much less a theater, it was difficult to imagine why they would want to be dressed as they were. Many wore thick cowls, dark, heat-absorbent robes which covered their whole bodies and perhaps had much to do with the odor which even Gantsch's insensitive nostrils could sense even from his elevated perch; the rest went completely stark naked without the least scrap of anything to protect themselves from the blistering rays of the midday desert sun. This struck Gantsch as somewhat odd, perhaps even intentionally self-destructive. He wondered if they were an escort of prisoners being punished for some horrible crimes against the welfare of the world, but even this failed to explain why occasionally one of the tortured souls would raise a fist or club and smite himself.

He had been watching this inexplicable procession for some moments when Balhudailadishtarya reappeared on the ledge and joined Gantsch in his observational lookout, shaking her head at the strange sight.

"Who are they?" asked Gantsch. "Dimpai don't usually..." He felt at a loss to explain how totally wrong this behavior seemed. "Do they?" he asked, to clarify, in case his assumptions were misplaced.

"Ascetics," Tarya replied in hushed tones. "They think pain is the only way to atone for sins and, you know, attain salvation; that whole bit."

"Why... They want to atone for evil deeds with self-torture?" he asked in astonishment.

"That's the general idea, yeah. I don't know which sect these guys belong to, but some actually believe that," she paused dramatically, "self-inflicted pain is its form of transcendence."

"I don't get it."

Tarya shrugged. "There are a lot of bizarre characters in the cosmos. These guys are pretty tame compared to some."

Gantsch watched the departing band with a look of subdued horror on his face.

"Don't get out much, do you, Sihvee?"

"Huh?"

Balhudailadishtarya pressed the advantage of her experience to shock her naive companion. "Those guys, not only do they torture themselves with the sun, their own fists and spiked clubs on special occasions, but they do ritual body piercings, they swallow various degrees of poisonous substances that burn out their insides without killing them, at least not immediately, and they ritually starve themselves." She let this sink in for a moment. "Of course, I've met people in cities who engage in most of those activities in the name of fun and fashion- they pierce themselves, swallow poisons and fast to get their figures to conform to a specific predetermined shape."

Gantsch considered this. When looked at in those terms, he had pierced himself and swallowed semi-poisonous substances; most of his friends at the university had done so as well. He had never been into the starvation thing, but he was reasonably certain that he had mated with females who were. He shook his head.

"So," he summarized, "they are taking society's activities to extremes as a symbolic gesture, in the hopes of bringing about some sort of atonement from the spirit world?"

Tarya made a quizzical raised-alien-eyebrow expression which the reader will have to imagine.
their little band aren't really sincere enough and will be condemned in the afterlife regardless."

She thought about this for a while, shaking her head. "Speaking of poisonous chemicals," she concluded, "I'm going to have a smoke, and then let's bugger on out of here."

Chapter 8: The Warlord's Henchmen

Gantsch had almost forgotten that they were actually on the way to anywhere in particular; he had become so caught up in the journey that it seemed unnecessary to have any sort of destination.

Apparently, he was alone in his absentmindedness. Everyone else had been looking forward to reaching the Gompa Oasis for days, and not just because of the fresh water. Two major trade routes intersected near the oasis, and much trading and social activity took place around the old stone ruins.

"We might be able to trade a few vebuthas for a dromi," someone suggested.

*   *   *

The Gompa Oasis has now become a holy site to many religions, for it is far from any other water source, and the rocky basin contains drinkable water year round.

Near the spring itself are huge ornate pillared stone ruins: all that remains of what was once a roadside rest stop. Like the other ancient ruins they had seen along the way, the landmark was part of a system of travelers' amenities along the long pan-peninsular transcontinental highway from Varum to Kiranesh, established by some forgotten monarch in the prosperous days of the Empire, before the Fire Wars. Gantsch and Sriaugh had seen many such markers along their journey; but this was the largest, most ornate rest stop they had seen yet. Even in ruins, the sheer scale of the palatial design was awe-inspiring; although the flames of war, followed by centuries of vandalism, disuse, and erosion, had left only a crumbling, roofless shell which merely hinted at its former grandeur.

Joyously the group approached the desert ruins, with the basin at the center that was filled with water even at the hottest time of the summer.

Just then, they were unexpectedly waylaid by a very different type of commerce than what they had expected.

Dangling a stinky cheroot from his lips, the pale skin of his face roasted to a fiery pink by the desert summer sun, his hair greasy and his clothing unkempt, a stranger, armed with a sword and backed by two fearsome companions, stepped in front of the approaching band of wandering Dimpai, and barred their way.

"It costs," said the foremost of the dirty bandits, and leered.

"Greetings," replied the chief of the Smyrna with great formal civility. "We are the Smyrna. Our people have wandered long in this broad desert. We have ventured forth with great courage, and after many days in the hot sun we have arrived here with a mighty thirst; and we are looking forward to refilling our water stores with the sweet waters of the Gompa Oasis."

"It costs," the foremost bandit repeated.

"And it costs more, every time you make him tell you again," said a faceless henchman.

"A lot more," piped up the other faceless henchman, again waving his really rather ridiculously oversized weapon, to make sure everyone had seen it.

"Is that so," sighed the chief of the Smyrna.

"Yeah," said the first henchman.

"It shouldn't cost anything," protested the Smyrna chief. "Water is a public resource. The Gompa Oasis belongs to no one."

"It costs!" the head of the bandits said again, starting to get annoyed.

"And if we tell you that you have to pay, then you have to pay; and anyone who challenges that, is looking for trouble!" said the other henchman.

"We're not looking for trouble," said the Smyrna chief, and paused to look at each of the three bandits in the eye.

"Good," said one of the henchmen. "I'm sure we can come to some arrangement."

"We're just here looking for water," said the Smyrna chief.

"Well, of course; that's what anyone comes here for, isn't it?" said the more talkative of the two henchmen. "I mean, there's no other reason anyone would come here... Out in the middle of the desert, it's hardly a destination in its own right."

"The warlord Kragston has declared himself ruler over all this territory," said the shortest of the three bandits in a self-important voice that would have been humorous if it had not been a serious threat. "All who pass through or partake of its resources must pay him homage."

"It costs," the leader explained once again.

"No one is the ruler of this territory," scoffed Chief Quithtar. "Look around you, man, it's a fuckin' desert!"

"Watch your tongue, woman, or we shall cut it out," threatened the second henchman, large, ugly, and heavily armed.

"Kragston is the ruler now," the chatty first henchman went on, "and those who challenge his authority tend to die painfully, so you'd best accept it!"

"I don't care if your boss-man declares himself the Grand Wahoo of the whole entire Universe," Quithtar tossed back. "*You* can lick his boots all you want, but I don't owe him shit. Now, get out of my way."

The chatty henchman turned his conversational grin into a scowl. "Where do you think you're going?" he asked the Smyrna chief, who was trying to ride her dromi around the bandits who were blocking the path.

"We're going to get water," explained the chief in a tone of voice which suggested that the fact of the matter should have been self-evident.

"But you haven't paid us," the short henchman reminded her.

"It costs!" screamed the leader of the bandits, who, though a man of few words, was possessed of an uncommon gift for focus and clarity of purpose.

"Indeed," replied the Smyrna chief. "So you have said." Quithtar made no further comment for a moment. "There's just one problem," she explained presently; and after another quite profound pause, she specified the problem. "We're not going to pay you."

"It co-" the uninteresting bandit leader said one final time, but never managed to finish the word and instead trailed off in a pained "-ooaaaaaaugh!" as a bright red stain appeared on his chest, a stain that rapidly grew darker in color even as his eyes lost their light and his awareness left him and his lifeless body slumped down to the well-trodden road of the dusty desert ground outside the oasis.

The strange humming sound of the weapon had come from beside him. Gantsch turned to see Balhudailadishtarya pointing an antique handheld vlastur at the bandits. She had her hand on the trigger, and had evidently just used the device to open up a hole that went clear through the chest of the lead bandit. The surviving two widened their eyes in terror as they saw her turn the device and point it at them.

"Don't shoot!" one said. In a flash he had grabbed Gantsch by the shoulders, and held him as a human shield. "You'll hit the Sihvee for sure!"

"Like hell," grumbled Gantsch, and flung his own weight backwards against this attacker. The man was strong, and he had the better grip, so that for a few moments after they had landed in the dust and struggled there for supremacy, Gantsch was truly fearful that he might have made a grave strategic error that might end in the fracture of his neck at any moment now. Nonetheless, through sheer force of cussedness, Gantsch was able to persevere.

With a last burst of energy, he swung his head backwards, and bashed his enemy full in the nose. This blunt force startled the attacker enough that Gantsch was able to wriggle free of the bandit's immediate grasp. Turning, feeling a tumultuous rush of panic and adrenaline elation at his near death and sudden triumph, Gantsch rode the wave of righteous fury and repeatedly smashed his downed opponent in the bloody face with a fist. Off to his left, he was dimly aware that one of the Dimpai warriors had speared the third and final bandit through the gut with one of the vebutha-herding poles, and the skewered rapscallion was sinking to the sand spurting his life's sustenance through a squishy search of his stomach.

The bandit who Gantsch was beating became aware of his comrade's demise as well, and attempted to bargain for his life.

"There's gold in our packs," he begged, burbling. "Take it, please..."

"We will, thanks," said Tarya. Then she aimed her weapon at the bandit's head, and put him out of his misery.

"Where did you get that vlastur?" asked Gantsch with open amazement. "It looks like an ancient relic."

"It is," said Tarya, showing it to him. "They haven't even made plastic like this since before the Fire Wars."

"And it's in such good condition!" Gantsch gawked geekily. "You can still see the original texturing stamp!"

"Yeah," agreed Tarya proudly, "this vlastur has been a family heirloom for many generations. It's very difficult to recharge the power pack anymore; we have to go to a certain Sihvee settlement outpost where they have the right kind of plugs at a charging station. There are few left like it."

"Absolutely," Gantsch agreed, "you're right, this baby is a rarity! I've seen one something like it, one time: it was a part of a collection, that was on display, you know, an exhibit at a museum; but yours is in much better condition. I don't think theirs would even fire!"

"This vlastur will vaporize rock at ten yards," Tarya said, not to boast, but just as a statement of power.

"You," said Gantsch in admiration, "are a very formidable woman."

"I am," Tarya agreed. "And don't you forget it."

Then this very formidable woman gave her bloody-knuckled man a very hot and heavy open-mouthed kiss to reward him for his bravery, and Gantsch knew in that moment that he was the luckiest man on the Mohaani Peninsula; no, scratch that: he was, in fact, the luckiest man on all of Extarus.

Chapter 9: The Holy Omasu Ceremony

That evening as the tribe sat around the fire, passing the phortawanay and telling stories, the elders announced to the company in general that an Unforeseen Holy Day would commence immediately.

*   *   *

Gantsch and Sriaugh joined the nomads for the ceremony they always performed when ingesting the Omasu. Gantsch liked the ceremony, with its ritual invocation of the Dimpai gods: the singing, the call and response ritual chants, the passing of the Omasu tea, the flowing way the Dimpai females danced after the drug took effect. Being near the oasis made them all feel secure and established a relaxed environment: an ideal communal frame of mind for communing with the Withinwithout.

*   *   *

Late that night, they sat around the fire in quiet companionship, admiring the flames.

"Combustion has an undeniable mesmerizing quality," said one.

"Watching things burn is captivating," agreed another.

"Huh, huh," chuckled Gantsch with a huge grin, amazed that his mouth could still move. "Yeah. Fire is cool."

Someone began thrumming a swift beat on a hand drum. Others joined in. Soon, many people were beating, tapping, even pounding on drums of varying shapes, sizes and sounds. Balhudailadishtarya played her vlayolasth. After a time Gantsch got out his vyolan. His digits seemed to have ideas of their own, they wouldn't do quite what he asked of them, but he liked the sounds they made as he sounded the strings with his bow. Every note seemed to mean something. The musical phrases invoked the sunset behind the ruins with the Rainbow Mountains in the distance and the sky incredible pastel hues. Gantsch's note lines crisscrossed in an ever-expanding pattern with the complex syncopated rhythms from the drummers.

Then Tarya started harmonizing her vlayolasth with his vyolan. They improvised a duet. Their notes danced around each other, they musically frolicked together, they played off of each other's ideas, they played with each other, they climbed musical mountains together and then came skipping all the way back down. The dancers went crazy, people started cheering; nobody could believe what was happening, least of all the fiddler and the piper.

As Gantsch and Tarya played, al-Bert suddenly burst into song. "I want to remind you all," Tarya's leathery-skinned father sang in a resonant ritual chant, "the words of the great prophet Rheild:

> "Everything is significant
> therefore nothing is significant;
> nothing is significant
> therefore everything is significant."

He sang it again, and other nomads began to sing along with him, until all the dancers and onlookers were singing and chanting:

> "Everything is significant
> therefore nothing is significant;
> nothing is significant
> therefore everything is significant."

Gantsch felt that the scene around him was utterly incomprehensible; the Omasu ceremony was so unlike anything he had ever experienced; he felt as if the exquisite beauty of this melodious chant was the most purely condensed ultimate truth he had ever encountered and that this moment was, for reasons he would never comprehend, the most important of his life.

Gantsch looked at Tarya. He could hardly believe that he was on good terms with such an extraordinary creature. He knew he would never meet another female to compare with her.

Tarya saw Gantsch looking at her. She looked back, for a moment. Then she smiled, raised the lucky vlayolasth to her beautiful lips, and played a melody on which they had been harmonizing earlier, as if to say, "come and play with me."

Gantsch joined in with his vyolan. As he played it he considered some of the concepts that Balhudailadishtarya had been telling him about Rheildism, and tried to incorporate that world view into his experience of each passing micro-moment. He tried to just let the music flow from his digits effortlessly, watching his fingers as they danced over the strings, listening as the sounds from his instrument danced around the sounds which Tarya produced from her vlayolasth.

The two of them danced around each other as their musical notes danced around each other. They played for hours before they stopped. They stopped quite suddenly and just stood there staring at each other. Nobody else seemed to realize that they had stopped. Some of the dancers were still dancing to the drums but most of the people had moved off in their own little worlds to do whatever, where ever.

*   *   *

Gantsch and Tarya wandered away from the fire circle together. Walking hand in hand, they passed beneath

Quithtar, who was seated motionless upon a large colorful boulder off to the side of the pathway.

Quithtar's immobile posture and her elevation above eye level rendered her nearly invisible; and indeed her trancelike state nearly precluded any notice of them, except that some words of their conversation drifted up to her where she sat.

"I've never felt that kind of musical connection before," a man's voice said.

"I've never felt *any* sort of connection like that before," answered the sultry voice of a young woman.

Quithtar smiled to herself at the obvious romance and sexual tension she could hear in these voices, then she began to wonder who the voices belonged to. Peering down into the darkness, she could just barely make out the receding forms of two young people: the Sihvee boy with the strange name, and a Smyrna girl; not just any girl, she finally realized, but her own daughter, Balhudailadishtarya. Quithtar sighed. Well, Tarya had long been old enough to go off alone with boys if she wanted to; in fact, Quithtar happened to know that Gantsch was not the first, nor the second for that matter. The Smyrna were not a prudish people, and youth was a time for exploration. This particular coupling could be problematic for the tribe later, if her daughter formed an emotional attachment to a Sihvee foreigner; but that was a matter to be dealt with in its own time.

Turning her attention back to the sky, Quithtar focused her inner eye on her spiritual connection with the Withinwithout.

Chapter 10: New Directions

The euphoric trance lasted a day and a night. After dancing and running in the desert sun in a holy vision-state for a long time, Gantsch slept the sleep of exhaustion resultant from temporary enlightenment.

The next day, Tarya's people packed up all their gear and prepared for another leg of their endless nomadic journey.

"So, where are you off to next?" Gantsch asked Tarya as he helped her fold up the tent where they had made love the previous evening. In truth they had already had a similar conversation, but he was clumsily trying to think of a way to change her answer.

"When we leave here," Tarya told him, "the tribe is heading south, to a certain place near the coast where people go to trade. From there, they intended to sell vebuthas at barter posts like this all the way up the coast, from Varum back to the Rainbow Mountains. After that, they'll probably go back through the pass to Scruggs, to reup the ceremonial Omasu supply, before heading back down south on the other side of the peninsula, following an ancient trade route that runs along the near side of the Rainbow Mountains. By the time they get to Kiranesh, it will be time to head back up towards Scruggs again, and the cycle begins anew."

"Wow," said Gantsch, who could not think of anything better to say. "That's a long way to travel."

"Yes, it is," agreed Tarya with a smile, "but if you just put one foot in front of the other, you'll get somewhere eventually. We're never in any real hurry. We bring most of the things with us that we need. This is just our way of life."

"It is a beautiful life," Gantsch said with cheerful heartfelt admiration. "I love these colorful tapestries."

"That one is woven from imported vlacks fibers by a cooperative of women in Varum. They hand-dye the prints using ink made from gargathod glands."

"How do you remove the glands from a gargathod?" Gantsch asked in wonderment.

"You cut it open," Tarya said matter-of-factly.

"So, the gargathod does not survive the procedure," reasoned Gantsch, who had never seen a gargathod.

"No," said Tarya, who felt as though she was explaining really obvious things to a young child, "not usually."

"So," Gantsch abruptly changed the subject, and somewhat nervously asked this beautiful exotic tribeswoman, "how would you like to go to Kiranesh and see how the Sihvees live?"

"I don't know," said Tarya truthfully. "Are you asking me to come home with you to meet your family?"

"Yes," Gantsch said, wondering why it is always necessary to state the obvious, "I would like that, please, if you would."

She hardly had to think about it. "I would love to," she said.

Most years, Tarya would have been excited to go on the journey south towards remote Kramwek with her people, and from there to high-society and sophisticated Varum. This year, her mind and her body were filled with excitement at the thought of very different plans.

"Well, he seems like a nice boy," Chief Quithtar said doubtfully, when her daughter informed her of her new plans. They were tending the vebuthas while al-Bert prepared the evening meal. "But are you sure he can protect you?"

"I'll be all right," Balhudailadishtarya told her mother confidently. "I have my vlastur, if anything goes wrong. I'll probably end up protecting him," she chuckled.

"It might be a long time before you can catch up with the tribe again," Quithtar worried.

"I know the trade routes," Tarya reassured her mother. "The Smyrna will be heading back towards Kiranesh in a few months. I can meet up with you then, or if I need to find you sooner, then I know how to find you, I promise."

"Well, if you're sure," said Quithtar, who was beginning to realize how much she would miss Tarya's bright smile.

"I'll see you soon," Balhudailadishtarya promised.

Meanwhile, Gantsch went back to his own camp to deliver the news to his friend and traveling companion from the University. "So hey, Sriaugh," Gantsch said, "change of plan, I guess I should tell you: Tarya is going to head back to Kiranesh with us, and like, I'll probably ride in her carriage most of the way, but we'll totally caravan, right?"

"Oh, ha ha," wild-eyed Sriaugh laughed, "things are going pretty well with her, huh?"

"Oh, uh," replied Gantsch, looking at his sand-covered feet, feeling embarrassed, "yeah, I guess..."

"Cool, cool," said Sriaugh, who did not particularly care. "Yeah, man," he said in a more businesslike tone, "if you have a ride with her, then you know, I might actually just head straight north from here."

"North?" asked Gantsch in surprise.

"Yeah, you know, I was thinking last night, during the Omasu ceremony, that Omasu is such a good thing; and now the Smyrna have told me where to find it, I was thinking I should head to Scruggs, and do a trade. After that, I'll head back to the Southeast Plains to hang out with a tribe called the Fifthers."

"The who?"

"No, the Fifthers."

"Who are they?"

"Some old friends of mine. They were these desert nomads for a long time, until they became herders; and now they live in the plains on the Southeast corner of the Mohaani Peninsula."

"I see."

"Yeah," Sriaugh went on, "believe me, you would like these guys. They're fucking crazy. And, hoo boy, their artwork is like *nuthin'* you ever seen." And he laughed a big loud laugh. "Those temples and shit they got down there... I ain't sayin' I *buy* it, but I do think it's pretty interesting, you know, some of it. They got some crazy ideas, those Fifthers do, and they take 'em pretty seriously, or they say they do. You never can tell about those guys." He gave Gantsch a twinkling look, and winked. "They really like Omasu, too; but it's really hard to get, all the way over there in the Southeast Plains, you know, so they're willing to pay a premium price for it."

"Oh, yeah?" This was the first time Gantsch had heard Sriaugh offer any insight into his private business dealings.

"Yeah," said Sriaugh, who suddenly had little else to say on the topic.

"Like what?" Gantsch pressed, because now he wanted to know.

"Well, one thing you may or may not know about them is that they are major producers of the highest quality phortawanay you will ever come across."

"I think I may be beginning to see where you're going with this."

"I think I will work out a barter," Sriaugh concluded. "Arrange a trade. You know, replenish my supply."

"My suspicions are confirmed."

"It will be good. You would like those guys."

"I'm sure I would," agreed Gantsch politely.

"So anyway," Sriaugh concluded, "I wasn't going to say anything, as long as you needed a ride back to Kiranesh, now that the Smyrna have hooked me up with a new dromi, to replace my poor dead one..." Sriaugh cleared his throat and wiped his eye at the memory of the dead dromi. "So yeah, if you can get a ride with that Dimpai chick instead, then I might just go ahead and head off on my own, and become a solitary wanderer for a while."

Gantsch wished him well, and the friends parted company.

*   *   *

That very night, Balhudailadishtarya set off at short notice with her newfound mate, traveling in the opposite direction from her family and everything she had ever known. She and Gantsch were off to visit his homeland, Kiranesh to the east, on the far side of the Rainbow Mountains, on the coast.

Balhudailadishtarya snuggled against Gantsch on the seat of the cart as he drove the dromi- not a difficult task as the road was almost totally straight, although obscured by sand in many places. She giggled, cooed and teased Gantsch as he lightheartedly joked and flirted with her. Their cart traversed the miles past the rocky outcropping that marked the path.

Chapter 11: The Revenge
of the Warlord Kragston

The principal moon was near the horizon and nearly full, casting its bright light from behind a big butte, which cast a long shadow across the desert plain. Ktliven was the largest and the brightest of the three moons of Extarus. The other two moons were really just glorified asteroids trapped in an orbit encircling the planet; but the principal moon was the size of a planetoid in its own right, and it illuminated the land at night, a bright glowing orb in the night sky; almost like a third sun.

Gantsch and Tarya admired the view.

*   *   *

The long days spent avoiding the sun gave them plenty of time for leisure. When they were not sleeping or making love, they would talk for hours on an endless variety of topics.

Sometimes Balhudailadishtarya would play upon her vlayolasth while Gantsch scribbled in his notebook, sketching and jotting down observations and thoughts and catchy phrases, recording the events of the day, his impressions of Dimpai society, the habits of vebuthas and dromis, and his own occasional attempts to compose really bad poetry. Of course, he didn't intentionally compose it to be really bad, it just turned out that way. Sometimes Gantsch would read his poems to Tarya, and she would listen attentively, and smile generously, and sometimes laugh in the wrong places.

"I have no formal training in literary criticism," Tarya told him apologetically when she saw that she had offended him, "but shouldn't high art focus on lofty ideals and transcendental nature imagery?" she asked somewhat pointedly.

To which Gantsch replied with a sigh, "Yes, ideally, I suppose it should."

"It's just that you've focused so much on that which is unpleasant: the intense heat, the sticky sweat, the stink of the dromi hide, the piles of smelly vebutha shit, and how hard it is to get vebutha shit off your foot if you accidentally step in some – these don't seem particularly transcendental to me... but what do I know?" she concluded innocently, trying to sound humble.

"You know a lot," he assured her quite literally, "and you're right, of course. These aren't the preferred imagery of the major poets, but... I'm trying to do something a little different," he explained lamely. "I want to show the gritty reality: the dirt and the stink, the pain and the futility, the death and decay; because all of this existence is just temporary, and we must practice non-attachment."

"You're beginning to sound like the great prophet Rheild," Tarya said dreamily.

"See, I've learned a lot from you," Gantsch agreed. "A true scholar learns from anyone and everyone, not just from stuffy ol' professors in academia."

Tarya chuckled and snuggled up closer.

*   *   *

The romantic moment and their quiet reverie were interrupted in an instant when a ferocious bandit and two fierce henchmen materialized out of the shadows and blocked the roadway. The bandits were riding armored dromis and shaking their shining sharp swords threateningly.

"You are the ones who killed Frengariko!" screamed the foremost bandit in a voice that was almost a sob.

The two young people looked at one another, perplexed. Gantsch shrugged his shoulders.

"We don't know who that is," Tarya informed the interlopers diplomatically.

"At the Gompa Oasis?" prompted the bandit.

Nobody said anything.

"What did he look like?" asked Gantsch.

"Did you kill more than one person at the Gompa Oasis?" insisted the bandit with outraged feeling.

Again, no one said anything for a moment.

"Well, come to think of it," said Tarya, "I guess we did, yes."

"So, one of the people you killed was Frengariko!"

"Not necessarily," said Gantsch, launching into a legalistic rationale. "If this Frengariko was anything like you, and he went around screaming his head off at total strangers over things they knew nothing about, then it's entirely possible that just about anyone and everyone he met might have wanted to kill him," he explained philosophically. "So therefore, it could have been anyone. You don't know it was us."

"You killed him over a paltry drink of water," the bandit accused. "Nothing more than a drink of water, and you thought that was worth a man's life!"

"Oh, I remember now," said Tarya in a lighthearted voice but with a frightfully stern look on her face. "Was that the guy who threatened to kill us if we refreshed our supplies from the Gompa Oasis?"

"All you had to do was give him a little something in exchange," the bandit insisted. "It wasn't so much. He was a reasonable man. He didn't want to take everything you had. He just wanted a little toll, to support him in his great work of protecting all the passers-by who visit the great Gompa Oasis."

"The water belongs to everyone," said the future chief of the Smyrna. Tarya had learned well from her mother. "No man may charge another to drink from the Oasis."

"The only thing your friend was protecting was his own interests," said Gantsch, "and we relieved him of that care. Now he won't have to threaten innocent travelers, ever again."

"You're not innocent!" raged the bandit. "You're murderers!"

"You're just describing yourself with those insults," said Gantsch. "Turning travelers away from an oasis in the desert, just because they refused to remit a ransom to a ruffian, would have killed them just as surely as any sword. Imagine if we had been traveling alone and unable to pay? What would he have done then?"

"Well, he'd have forced you into slavery, of course," said the bandit as though this was the most reasonable thing in the world. "Which is exactly what's going to happen now."

"And people allow this?" asked Gantsch, offended and dumbstruck.

"Who's going to stop us?" said the bandit belligerently. "The old Imperium has fallen. Kragston's word is the only law in the land, and he says you belong to us now. No one can stop us."

"We're going to stop you," said Tarya.

At that, the bandit finally lost his temper, and screamed in rage. The bandit's companions flanking him screamed in rage as well, and held out their weapons, preparing to charge.

"Get them!" roared the bandit. "Their freedom is forfeit. They shall be sold as slaves to suffer for their sins!"

"You should not have fucked with our friends!" screamed another henchman, and shook a fierce-looking blade in the air above his head.

"You still have that vlastur, right?" Gantsch nervously asked Tarya.

"Yeah, of course, I, it's right here," she said. Tarya tugged the tail end of the weapon and tried to take it out of her tote bag, but it seemed to be stuck. "I didn't want to give them too much advance warning," she explained, starting to sound worried.

"That's fine," he said as patiently as he could, "but I think maybe now would be a good time..."

"It's fucking stuck," she snapped, "and you're not helping."

"Sorry," Gantsch said defensively. "Okay, then." He looked up to see that they were surrounded by the smug soldiers of the anarchist warlord.

"Troubles?" asked one of the bandits with a sneer.

"Heh heh," said another, menacingly.

"No, no trouble at all," Gantsch lied. "We're just wondering what kind of slavery you had in mind."

"For *you*, Sihvee boy," said the one who seemed to be the group's leader, "we'll probably just put you in the mines. Kragston always needs more workers in the mines. The miners have an inconvenient way of dying, you see; so he always needs to replace them."

"Very dangerous place, the mines," said another, raising his eyebrows. "No safety standards."

"That does indeed sound dangerous," agreed Gantsch, wishing Tarya had shot them all by now. He was not at all certain that he would be able to talk his way out of this situation, and it seemed less and less likely that they would be able to fight their way out of the situation. He flexed his fist, wishing he had a large axe to swing at the nearest desert ruffian.

"And this is the great thing about a world without a central government of any kind," the bandit mused philosophically. "There are no laws to prohibit slavery; so a great man like Kragston is able to pursue his individual freedoms to the fullest extent of his imagination. You see, one man's freedom is never really complete unless he has the freedom to *take away* freedom from someone else; and that's the kind of freedom that Kragston covets more than anything: the freedom that formerly belonged to someone else. So, that's why he thrives in this anarchy. If he wants to take slaves, then there ain't nobody's going to stop him."

"Charming," commented Gantsch.

"And as for the little lady," the bandit continued, "she's good-looking enough for the brothels."

"You'll make a nice little piece of pussy," the largest companion informed her with a leer.

"You're disgusting," she told him, still struggling with the stuck sack. The vlastur seemed to be tangled in some clothing, which she was trying to surreptitiously remove, but

"I'll visit you there," the big henchman said, "and show you something truly disgusting."

"Give me that," said the third bandit, and snatched the satchel away from the surprised young woman.

"Hey!" she protested in frustrated rage.

"Oh, look, what do we have here?" asked the bandit leader, holding up the vlastur which Tarya had been on the verge of freeing.

"It's just a toy," Tarya lied.

"I think not," said the bandit. "This is a very valuable vlastur. They don't make 'em like this anymore. Kragston will be very pleased. Very pleased, indeed," he repeated, muttering to himself. "A man could defeat an entire army with one of these, just mow them down where they stand."

"It's mine, you fuck!" Tarya shouted, as surprised anger turned to despair.

"Not any more, it's not," said the bandit. "It's mine now, and so are you." To the other henchmen he said, "Take them away. Kragston will want to meet them before they are sold off."

"I'm not a fucking slave," said Gantsch, terrified that he was about to become a slave.

"You should have just paid for the water," the villain *tsked*. "It would have been so much easier for you. Now, somebody has to teach you a lesson."

With this, the largest of the henchmen punched Gantsch in the face. Gantsch wasn't expecting the blow, and went down, flopping like a fish, bruising his hand on a rock when he landed. He lay on the ground, curled up in pain, trying to bring his vision back into focus. He saw the giant henchman turn on the beautiful Balhudailadishtarya with a nasty leer in his eye.

Gantsch had spent the past several years studying old books in a hushed library, writing dissertations: contemplative analyses in which he compared and contrasted the benefits of various modalities of thought. He could recite from memory the sequence of events that had led to the Fire Wars and the fall of the old Empire, including not only the leaders of the nation-states involved, but also the secondary characters who had played such pivotal roles in inciting that great conflagration. This was his area of expertise. He had not spent much time training at fisticuffs.

Gantsch was a bit on the skinny side, not particularly well-muscled. He was a lover, not a fighter; and he was certainly no match for the trio of warlord's henchmen who had beset him and his lady-love on their journey. But as he watched the evil giant stalk towards Tarya, something inside Gantsch's brain snapped, and without thinking, he sprang from the ground and launched himself through the air with a howl of rage.

The bandit leader had turned with amusement to watch the largest henchman, who appeared intent on committing a brazen sexual assault right there in broad daylight. Gantsch tackled the leader bodily, and his momentum carried the man down to the ground, where he grunted in surprise, and lost his grip on the high-tech weapon in his hand.

The vlastur tumbled away between the rocks.

The other two henchmen turned to look in surprise as their leader struggled with the sedate Sihvee slave-boy, tussling and wrestling, each trying for a hand-hold.

The third bandit had approached and was about to reach into the fray and grasp Gantsch when Tarya, scrambling through the scree, managed to locate her precious vlastur, and brought it to bear. The bandit never knew what hit him. The vlastur's beam did not cause him to corporeally disintegrate, the way vlastur beams are depicted in some of the old science fiction movies; nor did it cause any portion of his body to explode, as satisfying as that might have been. The beam very simply, and quite quietly, opened up a gaping hole all the way through his head.

Still struggling on the ground, grappling Gantsch had no time to glimpse daylight through the warrior's wound; he was fighting for his life with the leader of the warlord's henchmen.

The largest of the trio, who had looked away from Tarya when Gantsch tackled the group's leader, now turned back towards her and advanced with renewed menace; but now Tarya was armed. She shot him through the chest, and left the beam on full for much longer than was probably strictly necessary. By the time his lifeless body collapsed to the sandy desert ground, most of his torso had been evaporated by the vlastur beam, and his head was nearly severed from his shoulders, flopping comically to one side, with a look of stunned surprise on his dead face as his lifeless, shredded corpse collapsed.

But it was all for naught! The small forgotten third member of the band of bandits had snuck up behind Tarya where she stood. Even as she watched the large bandit fall, the small one hit her over the head with a rock from behind.

Balhudailadishtarya fell to the ground, stunned, her eyes empty. The vlastur slipped from her grasp once again.

Gantsch ran rapidly to assist Tarya; but before he reached her side, he was intercepted by the group's leader.

Punched in the face, kicked in the belly, punched in the face again, and finally kneed in the genitals, Gantsch fell to the ground, unable to move.

"Well, *you're* a fighter," the bandit leader said to Balhudailadishtarya as she lay on the ground, still stunned from being struck with a stone. He ignored Gantsch, who had not earned the same distinction. "Now you've gone and killed Dubrowky," the bandit muttered, shaking his head. "Now I've got to take both of you to meet Kragston," he decided. "He'll want to meet you, I'm sure. Might have something special in mind for the Sihvee-Dimpai couple who are responsible for killing so many of his best officers."

"If they were his best – " Gantsch began; but without looking, the bandit leader kicked him in the face, and Gantsch rolled over in pain, tasting his mouth fill with blood.

"Shut up, if you have any sense of self-preservation," suggested the small bandit, who seemed a lot more talkative now that his larger colleague was lying dead on the ground.

Gantsch had little choice. The bandit leader had retrieved Tarya's vlastur from where it lay next to her on the rocky desert ground, and stood over them both as they lay injured and bleeding, pointing the deadly weapon at them while the smaller bandit tied them both up with very dirty rope.

The warlord's henchmen slung Gantsch and Tarya onto the floor of Tarya's carriage, and hitched her dromi to the back of their own carriage. After awkwardly manhandling their large deceased partially disintegrated and somewhat gooey companion's corpse into the forward carriage, the small one got in with the captives to serve as a guard, and the leader took the reins of the forward carriage, and the slave caravan set off to see the warlord.

Kragston, as it turned out, lived in the foothills of the Rainbow Mountains, a ways north of Aher Dahtl Dahl. This meant that, although the journey was far more uncomfortable than it should have been, captive Gantsch and trussed-up Tarya were following the same Imperial Highway eastward that they would have followed if they had not had the misfortune to encounter the warlord's henchmen.

The journey took two more days, during which time the captives were neither fed nor allowed to go outside to relieve themselves.

At night the henchmen ate in front of them, taunting them, "Oh, I bet you'd like some of this fresh-cooked vebutha meat, roasted over the fire, it's delicious, mmmm, you want some? Too bad! Ha ha hahaha!"

Without food or water, Gantsch's body had very little waste to excrete; but after enough time had passed, eventually nature took its course, and despite his desperate pleas, his captors steadfastly refused to give him even freedom enough to piss outside. Tarya's experience was similar in most key respects. By the time the carriage turned off the main road towards Kragston's compound, both of the unhappy captives' clothes were soaked in distilled piss, and they smelled awful.

From his vantage point on the floor of the carriage, Gantsch could not see what was going on outside; but he was aware that the little caravan had come to a halt, and that the lead henchman was speaking to someone outside. He decided later that this must have been the guard of the walled compound. After a brief conversation, the guard let them through, and the carriages rolled on.

A short time later, they came to a halt again, and without offering any explanation, the henchmen roughly tugged the stinky captives off the floor of the carriage and frog-marched them into the warlord's fortress, and down a dim hallway to the audience chamber.

Kragston the warlord was fat. It was difficult to notice anything else about him because his loathsome corporeal disgustingness was so remarkable. His bloated, swollen body stretched at his costly clothes. His cascade of extra chins completely obscured any vestige of what must have once been his neck. His face was all jowls, with a pervy mustache looking out of place on his upper lip. His fleshy fingers were so fat he could hardly grasp his fork, so he picked up hunks of roast vebutha with his hands, instead. His butt and belly were so big that he'd had to have a specially crafted chair constructed for him, a throne from which he could barely rise unassisted.

"So," Kragston addressed the captives when they were thrown to the floor before him. His voice was somewhat gargly owing to the greasy food in the back of his throat. He put down the hunk of fatty flesh he had been gnawing, licked his fingers, and wiped his mouth with the back of his hand, a procedure which failed to remove the smear of grease and sauce from his lips and cheeks. "You two are responsible for killing several of my men." He took a drink of purple veeno from a bronze chalice, and eyed the prisoners thoughtfully. "A Sihvee, traveling with a Dimpai princess," Kragston observed. "What brought the two of you together?"

Gantsch and Tarya said nothing.

"Probably a boring story anyway," Kragston said dismissively. "Anyhow, I can't have people like you interfering in my affairs," he informed them. "I've got to make you suffer for what you've done. You understand, it's nothing personal. I've got to make an example of you."

"Your henchmen tried to force us to pay to drink water from the Gompa Oasis!" Tarya erupted with rage burning in her eyes.

"Well, of course they did," said Kragston, who seemed to think he was the good guy. "I told them to. Everybody's got to make a living," he explained reasonably. "The oasis water is a valuable resource, so it only makes sense that people should have to pay to use it."

"But it's not yours!" Balhudailadishtarya objected. "The oasis belongs to all!"

"That fucking communist propaganda is such an outmoded way of thought," sneered Kragston derisively. "You can't just take water from me without paying for it. The oasis belongs to me, because I said so, and because I have armed warriors who are prepared to enforce my will. That's what being a warlord means. I don't believe in sharing, or community, or making the world a better place, or any of that shit. I believe in the right of the individual to take what he wants, and fuck anyone who stands in my way!"

"You seem like a really nice guy," said Gantsch sarcastically.

"I'm just misunderstood," said Kragston, sounding hurt. "See, what you fail to realize," the warlord explained, "is that the fall of the Empire created a power vacuum. In the absence of a central government, a state of anarchy exists; and when a state of anarchy exists, the world is just begging for men like me to take what they want by force, and establish themselves as the new rulers of the land. It's almost like I didn't have a choice," said Kragston, who had achieved his current position entirely through his own choices. "Anarchy breeds warlords, it's that simple. Warlords are, in fact, inevitable. If it hadn't been me, it would have been someone else; so it may as well be me!"

"I hope you die," said Tarya truthfully.

"I'm tired of this conversation," said Kragston the fat warlord. Motioning to a guard, he said, "Take these piss-soaked little shits out of here."

"What shall I do with them?" asked the guard. "Would you like them thrown in the dungeon?"

"I've been thinking about that," said Kragston contemplatively. "On the one hand, it would be satisfying to torture them to death and make an example of them. On the other hand, they have cost me a lot of money, between the men they killed and the water they refused to pay for. If I keep them in the dungeon, they will just cost me more money, between the jailers and the food and the torture master and whatnot. In order to recoup the losses they have caused me, I think the only realistic solution is to sell them into slavery, as soon as possible. This one," he pointed at Gantsch, "won't be worth much, but someone will probably find a use for him, working the irrigated fields out by the coast, perhaps, or more likely, down in the dangerous mines.

But this one," he turned a lascivious eye on the beautiful Balhudailadishtarya, "she'll fetch a small fortune. Someone will want her in his harem, I have no doubt. Her vagina has value. Clean her up a bit, and put her naked on the auction block. And make sure you don't skim off the top of the sales earnings," he warned the guard. "I'll know if you do."

"Of course not, sir," said the guard.

"Right. Now get them out of my sight."

Chapter 12: The Slave Market
of Aher Dahtl Dahl

The grumbling guard grumpily guided Gantsch and Tarya back through the grey corridors of the gaudy compound.

"Tell me to clean her up a bit," the guard scoffed, apparently confident that he would not be overheard by anyone who mattered. "Like I'm some kind of fuckin' washer woman or something."

Their hands were bound, and the guard was well-armed, as he repeatedly reminded the captives by poking them in the back with his sword. Gantsch gazed at the glorious wide-open open sky, bright with the daylight of his last day of freedom, he thought with despair, as he tried not to think of being sold at the market. He tested his bonds, but his hands were bound tight. He looked left and right, but the narrow corridor offered no avenues of escape, and when it opened up into the courtyard, there were more armed guards stationed at every corner.

"I'm sorry," Gantsch said sadly to beautiful Balhudailadishtarya. "I got you into this, and I don't see a way to get out."

"Don't give up yet," she said softly. "Watch. Be ready."

"Okay," he agreed with silent surprise, although privately he wasn't sure what he was to be ready for, or what opportunity could possibly present itself while he was bound.

"Tell me not to skim off the top," the guard was muttering to himself. "As if there's any other way of getting paid around here."

Tarya noticed that the guard elected to eschew assistance. Rather than requiring another guard to accompany him, the guard chose to take them to the market alone, "Probably because he does not wish to share his earnings," Tarya speculated silently, "and he probably assumes that because he is armed and his prisoners are bound, that he does not require help controlling them." This, she knew, was to be her opportunity.

But the guard was standing close behind her, and she knew he would overhear any whispered hints or plans, so she said nothing.

The guard shoved them back inside the filthy carriage, which smelled even worse than Tarya remembered, and bound their legs. This came as a disappointment to Tarya, who recognized that bound feet posed a serious impediment to her escape plan; but she tried to hold her feet apart, just a little, and as she had hoped, the guard was somewhat careless in tightening the bonds. Gantsch meanwhile was not thinking much of anything, he had given in to despair. The guard grumbled about the smell of the carriage – "Phew! What a fucking awful stench" – then locked the carriage door from the outside, still grumbling, "Burning in the hot fucking direct sunlight will be better than sitting in there with those…" and his voice trailed off as he climbed atop the carriage, still reciting a litany of foul words.

As soon as the unseen dromi began pulling the prisoners out of the compound, Tarya began squirming in her fetters.

"I can't reach my feet," she said, "but I think the ropes should be a little bit loose."

"Let me see if I can get to them," said Gantsch. He squirmed through the puddles of piss on the prison carriage floor, and awkwardly turned his body until he could reach the ropes that bound Tarya's feet. Unfortunately, his hands were behind his back; so as he attempted to untie her, he was facing away from her, working backwards and unable to see what he was doing. He had several false starts where his attempts to loosen the knots only ended up making the bonds tighter. At last through trial and error and pure dumb luck, he managed to loosen the knot, and began awkwardly tugging on the bonds, eagerly, a bit desperately, increasingly frantically, until at last she was able to kick them loose.

"Shouldn't I be working on untying your hands, instead?" he wondered aloud.

"You can try it now," she told him, "but the ropes on my feet were looser, so I figured we'd start where you had the best chance of success."

"Huh," he said, "okay."

But they had already reached the outskirts of Aher Dahtl Dahl, a lawless frontier settlement whose citizens walked armed down the street; although the prisoners couldn't see that from within the carriage.

Gantsch's grip on the ropes slipped as the carriage dipped and tipped and turned. They rattled and banged down winding lanes, in places so narrow that the carriage scraped the walls on either side several times. Gantsch and Tarya were thrown against one another, rolled around on the filthy floor, and tossed up against the carriage walls and even into the undersides of the unoccupied bench seats, as the dromi careened down the alleyways, the carriage wheels bouncing and jostling and making a great deal of noise as they rolled over the rutted streets of packed dirt and loose stones.

Abruptly the dromi pulling their carriage drew to a halt. Tarya braced herself as the guard unlocked and opened the door. "All right," he said, "let's get you – "

Though exhausted and starved, feeling weak, her hands still bound, Tarya kicked upwards with her legs, striking the guard in the chest so hard that he staggered backwards. It wasn't much of an opening, but it was enough.

Feeling off-balance with her hands tied behind her back, Tarya bent double and charged forth from the carriage, striking the guard with her head as he tried to rise back up from her earlier blow.

"Ow, hey, what the fuck!" the guard complained, not seeming to realize what was happening; but then he figured it out. Letting fly with a lengthy list of obscenities, he hastily slammed the carriage door shut and locked it once again before setting off in pursuit of the fugitive Tarya.

She ran as fast as she could, drawing curious stares and even a few mocking catcalls from the locals as she scurried down the street with her hands tied behind her back. She knew that their noise would give away her location when the guard came looking, so she had to get off the main streets and away from whatever market square played host to the slave auctions of which Kragston had spoken.

Stumbling along, she found a dark passageway between two buildings, and dropped down behind a disregarded trash pile, hoping her passage had been unremarked.

When she didn't hear the sounds of pursuit within a few minutes, she tried to calm her breathing, and began digging through the trash for anything sharp enough to free her from her bonds. At last she found a rough rusty nail, dull with age and not at all adequate to the task, but she had been searching for some time and hadn't found anything else useful, so the dull nail would have to do. With one end of it she scratched at the ropes and tried to part the threads, working her way through them with friction and sheer force of will. It took forever, as she fought down the rising panic that the guard would find her at any moment. But he must have already run right past her hiding place and missed it; he had been just behind her, he couldn't be that slow.

Time slowed to a crawl as she listened fearfully and worked furtively to break through the band of rope encircling her wrists. At last she felt the fibers begin to weaken and a surge of hope filled her with lightness; but then a voice behind her said, "What you doin' there?"

In a panic, Tarya tugged at the remaining rope, and with relief felt it give way at last, although the effort was quite painful and left burning bruises on her wrists. Trying to pretend that she had not just made her escape from certain sex-slavery, Tarya turned to face the stranger and said, as casually as she could, "Can't a girl take a piss in privacy around here?"

The stranger laughed. "Most folks prefer the outhouse, down the way, yonder," he said, pointing.

"It stinks," Tarya guessed, and when the man didn't disagree, she went one further. "There's flies."

The man guffawed even louder this time. "Welp, can't disagree with that," he admitted, and to Tarya's surprise, he turned and walked away, leaving her alone.

Hastily she hurried down the alley, peeked around the corner in both directions, and when she didn't see the guard anywhere, set off at a stroll down the sidewalk just as if she belonged there. A few people gave her strange looks, because most of them knew each other, whereas she was a stranger from out of town, with the dark skin and exotic clothing of a Dimpai, beautiful yet strangely disheveled and kind of rumpled and stained; they did not know what to make of her. She did her best to ignore the stares, and for the time being, no one said anything to her.

Cautiously staying near the walls and corners, Tarya tried to look down all the roads at each intersection without being really obvious about the fact that she was looking around at each intersection. She still didn't see the guard. Finally she got back to where she had left Gantsch in the dromi cart, and she realized why.

The cart was empty. Gantsch was gone.

The guard had evidently given up her pursuit, and instead had taken her boyfriend to the slave market alone. Tarya cursed softly to herself. How would she find him? She had to get to the slave market and stop the sale, or else... She could not imagine what would happen. There was no way she could rescue him after he had been sold. Gantsch would be gone for good. Such a fate was too horrible to consider. Though she had lived all her life wandering the deep desert with her people, she was familiar with the rumors of the deadly mines, where even the strongest slaves did not last long. A skinny Sihvee boy accustomed to the classroom would lack the strength to survive for long down in the dark, breathing the foul air that sometimes leaked poison gas out of the ground. The mines, she knew, were the source for not only precious minerals and gemstones, but more importantly, for the special construction materials still so prized by arrogant architects and bellicose builders whose work wished to hearken back to the styles popular in the great monuments constructed in the late days of the fallen Empire. The wealthy aristocrats who commissioned the construction and enjoyed those edifices were unconcerned with ethical sourcing practices for the raw materials. Such considerations had long ago fallen by the social wayside, in a land with no laws.

Tarya could not conceive of a plan to rescue the unfortunate Gantsch. In despair, she considered fleeing on foot. If she could escape from Aher Dahtl Dahl into the empty desert outside the settlement, she would be able to forage and hitchhike until she could catch up with the Smyrna tribe: her people, her roaming home; her mother and her father, Quithtar and al-Bert. She longed for the relative safety of returning to the tribe. After all there was little more she could do here now. She had no real choice. There was no realistic way she could rescue Gantsch at this point. She felt sorry for him, she really did, but what could she do? Any attempt to secure his release was doomed to fail and would almost certainly result in her own recapture and eventual sale into unspeakable horrors, a lifetime of torment as a sex slave for some disgusting pigman. It was not to be contemplated.

She sighed. She could tell herself all the excuses, she knew, but she and Gantsch had come here together. If she abandoned him to his fate now, she would remember it her entire life, and she would never forgive herself.

What then? She knew not what was to be done in this impossible impasse.

She was about to abandon the cart when she spied a familiar case lodged in the corner. It was the protective covering for her own vlayolasth. How it had come to be here was unclear; her kidnappers must have moved it when they moved her. Regardless, there it was, her most prized possession, the musical instrument that defined a substantial portion of her identity.

Dazed and uncertain, Balhudailadishtarya slowly walked down the dusty streets of Aher Dahtl Dahl, trying to think of a solution to this intractable issue.

Chapter 13: The Uncivilized Sihvee Outpost

As Balhudailadishtarya wandered the lonely streets of Aher Dahtl Dahl, vlayolasth in hand, she saw a man bolt out of a building, swinging the slatted double doors of the saloon as he exited. He caught her attention because he was running bent nearly double, which seemed to Tarya like a very strange posture for running. Tarya stared, intrigued, as the man stopped, kicked some dust, reached down swiftly and picked something up; then ran off behind a building. Moments later two more males ran out through the same swinging door bent in the same position, proceeded to amble about briefly, meanwhile raising a huge cloud of dust, and appearing to have reached a conclusion, followed in the path of the first.

"What peculiar behavior," thought Tarya to herself.

There must be an explanation, she was sure; but what sort of moral transgressions the tableau might imply, she was uncertain. *Let it remain a mystery*, she thought. She didn't really want to follow them, so she set off in the other direction, down what appeared to be a major thoroughfare, although there was not a lot of traffic about at the moment.

She presently became aware of a peculiar odor. She identified the source of the odor as the open sewer next to the path on which she was walking. "They have a poor sense of sanitation around here," she thought. "I quite think I shan't want to stay long."

Nonetheless, she continued to walk into the center of town. That, she thought, was where she was most likely to find the slave market; and therefore, it was the most likely place for her to rescue Gantsch.

But the town square, when she found it, was nearly deserted. Nobody else was there, except for a thin beaky fellow who watched her hawkishly. Tarya, remembering that ridiculous-looking characters can sometimes be quite dangerous, had to struggle with herself, to repress the urge to laugh out loud.

She tried to ignore him while keeping an eye on his movements; but after staring at her for a while, he appeared to have reached some decision, and walked over to where she was standing. As he approached, she bent to one side and swiftly snatched up a stone in her hand.

"You have a nice body," the stranger said.

She looked at him sidelong. "Thanks," she said flatly. *Creep*, she thought. She noted that he was still out of arm's range and hefted the stone. She would have to hit him at just the right angle, with impeccable timing, so that she could still move it fast but also so that when it came into contact with his head it would impact with a satisfying *thud*.

"How about you and me..." he said but didn't finish the proposition.

Tarya turned to face him, weighing the rock in her hand. *Now just one step closer, you son of a gargafli,* she thought.

"I'll pay you," he offered.

Tarya was so surprised that anyone would ever say this to her that she had to think about it for several seconds to be sure that she was understanding exactly what he was talking about. She knew that there were parts of the land where goods were exchanged for flattened pieces of metal, but the Smyrna only bartered, and... and if she was understanding him correctly, and from the look on his face she could not construe the situation otherwise, this Sihvee wanted to give her flattened pieces of metal in exchange for... for MATING with her. She laughed in his face, mirthlessly, and raised the jug ever so slightly.

"Here," he was saying. "Look at this. It's very rare. The egg of a jen-yoo-ine Fittlerof on the Peninsula. These eggs are very tough, survive lots; it made it all the way over the Peninsula mountains and across the desert and here it is, beautiful, durable, very valuable, very very valuable, and yours for just a few minutes with yours truly." He stepped forward. "They'll be the best few minutes of your-"

He was compelled to leave off at just that point in his sentence, for at that moment Tarya was very satisfied to hear a resounding clonk from his hollow head when she struck it with the stone; and the splat that his egg made when it hit the ground.

She kicked him. He rolled onto his back, stunned but conscious.

"Your egg is a phony," she said, "and so are you."

Disappointed with this sample of Sihvee life, she moved on, still seeking some sign to indicate how she might rescue her man in distress.

As she traveled down the street, she smelled something that made her stomach growl. The stench in the gutter was not as bad here, and the smell of cooking and brew came from one of the buildings. It had been a very long time since she had had a well balanced meal, and she knew it. She badly wanted to eat whatever was making that smell.

She had hardly entered the building when another male started behaving overly familiarly towards her. This one called her by entirely inappropriate endearments and made insinuating faces. She noticed that there were other people of both genders in the establishment and decided she had little to fear from this one, although he was kind of annoying.

"You bug," she informed the man disdainfully.

"Buzz," he said. "Hey do you play that?" he asked suddenly and pointed at her vlayolasth.

"Of course. That's why I have it."

"Let's hear."

She was about to refuse flatly when a thought occurred to her.

"Only if you dance," she said.

He was intoxicated, bored, open to suggestions and trying to impress the strange foreign female.

"Okay."

So she pulled out her vlayolasth, considered which of the songs she knew was the easiest to dance to, decided not to think about it for too long and started just making things up. The male looked surprised for a moment, then began to move his body in what he supposed was a seductive sway, although it was more of a grotesque unsteady wobble. Another male, watching this from across the room, burst into laughter and crossed over to where Tarya was playing to show the first how dancing was supposed to be done. Others noting the attractiveness of the musician and deducing that the dance was some kind of competition for her, joined in. Soon almost everybody in the establishment was grooving to her tunes.

"This is bloody strange," she thought to herself.

She thought it was even stranger when they started whooping. That's right, the males took turns seeing who could yell the highest and loudest. They had to live up to the name of their town.

She literally jumped when she felt the hand on her arm, but when she looked to see who the hand belonged to it was the friendliest face she had seen all day.

"Ever been a bartender?" said the woman.

"A what?"

"Let me put it this way. Would you like to be employed? You know, a job? You just made this whole place dance. I will personally pay you to stay, and all you have to do is pour a little brew in some glasses and play on that thing fer me an' my customers, regular like."

Instead of replying directly, Tarya said, "You really should do something about these open sewers. They are disgusting."

"Oh it's old Roester again, ma'am," said the bartender woman, "I keep telling him not to go in public but he'll be damned if anyone will tell him what to do, and being a desert man and all..."

"But more than one person's been doing it," Balhudailadishtarya observed noncommittally.

"Yes, well Roester is... he's respected in this community, and a lot of folks tend to do, well, pretty much what he does, you know..."

"You know, what I really need," Tarya told the bartender woman, "is not a job: I need directions to the slave market."

The woman glanced at her in suspicious surprise. "Doesn't seem like a nice place for a girl like you," she observed keenly. "Full of unsavory characters."

Returning the stranger's appraising glance, Tarya decided to trust her. It was a risk, but she needed help. It was a risk she would have to run. "My friend is there," she explained.

"Oh," said the bartender, her expression becoming less friendly as she appeared to reach a derogatory opinion of Tarya's character. "Well, then," she said, "I suppose it's the right place for you after all."

"No, you don't understand," Tarya said desperately, for now she knew that this woman was trustworthy, at least in regards to the question of whether Tarya herself should be sold into slavery. "He's being sold at the slave auction. I have to find a way to rescue him, or else he will have to go die in the mines."

"Ooooooooh," exclaimed the bartender in surprise as she understood the situation. Her evaluation of Tarya restored to a positive opinion, she nodded her head, then glanced back and forth secretively. "Not a good place for that discussion, out in the open here," she confided in a low voice. "Come with me."

"So," the bartender woman asked presently, "has anybody told you about Aher Dahtl Dahl, yet?"

They were inside the saloon, in a dark corner. It smelled of spilled beer and worse, but at least the poor lighting offered a degree of anonymity for their private conversation.

"You mean," Tarya asked, "have they told me anything other than, that there's a slave market here, and all the people who live in the town are okay with that?"

"Not everyone is okay with it," the woman said sternly, "but what are we going to do? The people who profit from the slave trade are organized and armed, and the people who have moral objections to it are not. But that," she continued, "is not what I meant."

"Fine," said Tarya a bit impatiently. "What did you want to tell me about Aher Dahtl Dahl?"

"I wanted," said the woman, "to tell you what its name means."

"And what does its name mean?" pressed Tarya, impatient with herself for even asking this.

"The settlement's name," explained the woman in a humorous voice, "means, 'the town when men cry out often,' in reference to the boastful yodel preferred by a certain style of vebutha ranchers."

As if to demonstrate her point, a high-pitched man's voice resounded from outside, 'round the corner and down the lane: he yodeled a piercing shriek that echoed through the night like the howl of some half-starved, loneliness-crazed voolf that had become separated from its pack in the remotest part of the Rainbow Mountains.

"Just like that!" exclaimed the woman brightly.

"I see," said Tarya doubtfully. "Vebutha ranchers, huh?"

"Ah-yup," the woman confirmed. "This here town is peopled by a rowdy bunch o' characters, all right. Why, sometimes they even like to torment vebuthas, just so's they can sit on the snouty beasts' backs, while the enraged creatures jump up an' down in anger and agony to try to shake them off."

"Seriously?" asked Tarya doubtfully.

"Oh, yeah," the barmatron averred. "The menfolk have these big ol' contests called rudhayos, where they try to see who can sit on the back of a rampaging vebutha the longest. Why, it's a major public event. Folks go there in droves."

"That's... very interesting," said Tarya insincerely.

"So," asked the other woman, who still had not introduced herself, "what ya want ta get mixed up with the slave traders for?"

"It's a long story," said Tarya.

The bartender sighed and shook her head. "I was just trying to make conversation," she said. "Of course I'm going to help you, but I'd like to know what you're facing."

"Well, my, uh, my boyfriend," Tarya explained. She had never used the word aloud before. "Gantsch," she specified. "We were kidnapped by the warlord Kragston, and now Gantsch is going to be sold at the slave market here in Aher Dahtl Dahl."

"Ya shoulda mentioned that last bit," commented the other woman, "at the beginning of the conversation."

"I didn't know if you were going to hand me over to him!" protested Tarya.

"You what?" asked the barwoman, looking offended. "Do I look like..."

"I just don't know anyone here," Tarya explained.

The woman sighed. "Fair enough," she allowed. "You're probably feeling well out of sorts: a stranger in a strange land, as they say. And the circumstances that brought you here probably don't instill you with a lot of trust towards the people who live here. I can understand that. But believe me when I say, I'm on your side and I want to help you. That bastard Kragston thinks anarchy means the rule of the powerful, and no legal guarantee of rights for the many."

"But," objected Tarya, "that *is* what it means."

"No, you're thinking of Libertarianism. Anarchy is like that, only with more fire."

The sound of crashing bottles could be heard on the street outside, followed by nearby cries of "Fire! Fire!"

"Right on time," the bartender woman told Tarya, her voice rising. "That will keep the slave market's security people busy for a few minutes."

"The market?" asked Tarya hopefully.

"The slave market is right around the corner," explained the bartender woman, who seemed to be in no hurry to divulge her identity. "Let's see if we can go rescue your boyfriend in distress."

"Actually," said another voice, as a figure stepped through the swinging double doors of the saloon, silhouetted by the setting sun outside, "before you go, maybe you should gather some more allies."

Tarya looked towards the unexpected figure. "Mom?" she asked in bewildered surprise.

"I couldn't *really* allow my daughter to wander off unsupervised," admitted Chief Quithtar as she entered the saloon. "Not that I followed you, I didn't!" she immediately protested, then clarified, "but I did send a couple of scouts after a while, just to make sure you got where you were going; and when they found your dromi... well, we came as fast as we could."

"I'm so glad to see you," gushed Balhudailadishtarya, and wrapped her mother in a warm embrace.

"Me, too," said Quithtar. Then she stepped back and looked Tarya full in the face. "And," she said, "we brought weapons."

And that's how a small underground band of freedom fighters led by the owner of the local tavern came to be joined by a well-armed tribe of matriarchal nomads; and together, they launched an all-out assault on the slave market in the outpost town.

The paltry security force at the marketplace was only meant to restrain the bound or shackled slaves on the auction block; the guards withered before the onslaught of the combined force of attackers. The slaves, once rescued, joined their rescuers for a revenge march on Kragston's compound.

It took time to walk the dusty road from the outpost village to the warlord's compound. They passed the time making up songs about all the creative ways they intended to dismember Kragston and his cohorts.

But they had not yet reached the compound when three bandits startled them when they stepped out into the roadway, blocking the group's passage.

"Stop right there!" commanded the first bandit.

"Turn around," chimed in a second.

"And go back where you came from," finished the third.

The Smyrna smirked at this, for they greatly outnumbered the bandits. Feeling themselves a strong army, they prepared to meet the puny feeble attempt at an onslaught; until they heard a sound, and they stopped, and looked around, and realized that they were surrounded on all sides by more bandits.

"What, you thought there were only three of us?" sneered the first bandit.

Gantsch shrugged, and off to his left he noticed that the chief shrugged, as well.   "Yup," he said, "I guess we did."

"Well, more fool you!" said the bandit. "Prepare to die! The deaths of the martyrs shall be avenged!"

"I can't believe you actually believe you're on the right side of a righteous fight," Gantsch said to the bandit, and shook his head.

"Attack!" screamed the bandit, undaunted.

"Quick," Balhudailadishtarya said to Gantsch in an undertone, "look, about forty-five degrees off to the right."

Kragston had confiscated her vlastur, and she was really missing it right now, but Tarya was determined to make the best of the situation.

Gantsch looked ninety degrees off to the right, checked behind him, looked left, looked forward, and finally figured out where she wanted him to look.

"There's a weak spot in their line, there," Tarya indicated, trying to ignore Gantsch's folly.

"Where there's that one small guy?" asked Gantsch, to show he was paying attention.

"Yes, that guy," confirmed Tarya. "He's just little, and the line around him is spaced out too far. The guys on either side won't be able to come in to his rescue in time, if we take him out; and then we'll be through their line."

"Then take him out we shall," said Gantsch. Then, raising his borrowed blade, he let fly a throaty war cry, and charged forward with all his might. Turning aside from the well-armed threesome who had first accosted them, Gantsch and Tarya focused the full force of their attack on the solitary smallish soldier.

"Holy fuck, this short guy is ripped," Gantsch noticed in admiration; but it was too late to get worried about his target's musculature.

Dashing into the fray, Tarya was already swinging her morningstar at the man's middle.

The bandit was already twisting to meet her attack. He brought his shield about with one arm and raised his sword arm at the same time. This threw him slightly off balance.

That was all the opening Gantsch required. Past the soldier's defenses he deftly slid his sword, forcefully yet smoothly, as if the weapon was making love to the bandit's throat. The sharp edge parted skin, flesh, windpipe, and jugular, instantly disabling the man and dropping him to the ground.

Now that they were through the line, Gantsch and Tarya quickly turned about to scan for advantage. They saw their comrades engaged in fights on both sides. One of the fights was a large melee, with many participants all lashing about. On the other side of the battle was a small skirmish between just one or two people.

"Let us join the melee," suggested Gantsch, "that we might win the greatest victory."

"No, not yet," Tarya stopped him just as he was about to charge into the midst of the fray. "Let us first intervene in the smaller fight. Once that is settled, we will have another ally with us as we charge into the larger fight."

"You sound so wise," said Gantsch in admiration.

"Why, thank you," said Balhudailadishtarya with a smile. "And I didn't even go to some fancy school like yours!"

"Hey, there's no need to act all jealous," he said.

She sighed. "Let's talk about this later," she suggested.

Gantsch nodded. "Yeah, all right."

Turning to the smaller fight, they joined forces with the Smyrna beset by bandits, and quickly bested the bastards. Then, just as Tarya had predicted, those friends joined them as they rushed toward the melee on the other side of the battlefield.

The warlord's henchmen didn't stand a chance.

The Beginning

Epilogue

Gantsch emerged from his tent groggily. He wrapped a thin scarf wrapped around his face and head. Gantsch always did this when he had to go through this part of the desert. The scarf kept the sand out of his eyes and breathing orifices; it reduced the glare of the sun; and if it interfered with his sense of smell, that was all right, because there was nothing to smell except Cruiser the dromi.

He checked the solar collectors he had set up the previous evening. Since sunrise they had been focusing Dworon's fusion power on a water jug. The reflectors had been a gift from his mother-in-law, and they turned out to be a prized possession on these long journeys overland. The reflectors had done their work well; his jug was hot to the touch. He opened its stopper and mixed ground seeds of the qafay plant into the hot water. He rummaged through a pack until he found some tough dry bread, with which he exercised his teeth, jaw muscles and digestive system. He drank off the qafay in a peaceful mood, then took down his tent and packed it into a pack. Finally, he strapped the packs and water jugs to Cruiser, his dromi, whose digestive bladders indicated that the incredibly hardy rintsyan plant which she ate thrived in all areas of the desert: even all the way out here. He climbed up onto Cruiser's back and pointed her in the direction they would travel until the sun got too high in the sky. Cruiser began the odd six-legged scurrying motion which with she traversed the sand. Gantsch unwrapped his head scarf and observed the ritual phortawanay pipe sacrifice to the Sandstorm Gods, imploring them to grant him safe passage. Gantsch wasn't really sure he believed in the Sandstorm Gods, but he believed in deadly sandstorms, and he rather enjoyed the phortawanay pipe sacrifice ceremony; so he figured, if there were some sort of invisible beings controlling the weather out here, it was just as well to be on good terms with them.

Through the years, Gantsch had grown so accustomed to the dromi's rancid smell that he needed no carriage, but sat directly on her back in his travels: rocking back and forth with the giant lizard's swaying motion as he perched amidst the jugs, bags, bundles, and baskets of miscellaneous stuff that constituted all his property in the Universe.

Gantsch and Cruiser, his only traveling companion, followed no roads, frequenting high places where they scampered over rocks and the wind blew his hair from his sunburned face. He secretly prided himself on his image but would have been mortified if anyone had accused him of doing so.

Gantsch coughed and reflected on the positive aspects of solitude. Company was nice, sometimes; but it was a good thing to be alone, even if your only companion is a gigantic smelly beast whose only talent for verbal communication consists of the occasional hiss and an even rarer bellow.

Gantsch surveyed the pass.

He was no stranger to this road, for it was the only path to and from the Foreign Trading Post in the underground city of Scruggs, carved out of the living rock deep in the north face of the Rainbow Mountains in the southernmost part of the Nawathian Mainland.

Gantsch had traveled this way many times, but the wise traveler never allowed himself to feel comfortable in such an environment: he must always be on his guard, for the pass was dangerous, the mountains treacherous, and the weather unpredictable. The possibility of avalanche was the most glamorous fear, but the weather was the greatest danger, for the avalanches, ice-storms and sandstorms of the region had a 100% mortality rate for travelers caught in them.

Gantsch looked ahead. The scene was indescribably incredible- the mountains, their cliffs, crags, crevices, crevasses, canyons- and he was almost all the way to the top. He was enjoying the full splendor of one of those natural focal points of the Withinwithout; he was at the center of a mind-bogglingly vast expanse of incredibly intricate landscape, the shapes and colors of the geography infinitely varying, infinitely subtle, worked on such a huge scale... He reflected that not even a large dose of the powerful Omasu he had brought back from the pale-skinned cave-dwellers in the north could produce splendors on such a grand scale.

The wind was blowing Gantsch's hair quite picturesquely, and his descent into the foothills of the Rainbow Mountains involved a number of dramatic scenery changes; but he was too pestered and perturbed to enjoy it. He couldn't remember doing anything that would offend any of the Dimpai gods, yet the pestilence which plagued him today seemed like their vengeance. (It only seemed so to Gantsch because he was disturbed; any real Dimpai would have said it was merely the peevishness of a spirit, as the wrath of one of the gods would have been much, much worse.) Gantsch felt the tickling sensation as another one landed on his leg. He let it sit there just long enough to start feeling safe, then crushed it, shaking its slimy innards from his hand onto the desert sands. He cursed in some foreign tongue. He didn't know what these things were, but he did know they were really ruining his morning. They were just a little bigger than his smallest digit and they could fly. Flicking them off was useless because they just came back, and if he tried to ignore them they always bit him eventually. At least they didn't seem to inject any poison, he thought, looking on the bright side. They almost seemed to be simply nibbling on him out of curiousity; but that thought did not make the sensation of their mandibles entering his flesh any more pleasant.

Gantsch eventually remembered some half-comprehended tales he had heard of travelers harassed by swarming things called Buking Fiters. At the time he had not really believed the stories about the cumulative effect of the swarms, stories about small animals and unattended children picked clean to the bones. He shook his head, again, hoping he didn't have any in his hair. He didn't need this. This whole being-someone-else's-lunch thing just totally offended his sensibilities. Gantsch decided in favor of an an early and extended lunch break.

"We deserve it," he explained to Cruiser. "First we got up early, and hit the road, and then we crossed some pretty rough terrain there, and then those..." and he proceeded to colorfully describe the hungry Buking Fiters, who weren't really to blame as they were small enough to be totally brainless and were therefore simply following their genetic instruction manual.

He picked a rocky outcropping off by itself as a likely site for shade and a picturesque place to chill for a couple hours. He was pleased to find, on reaching it, that a road ran by it. He followed no roads, but they were useful landmarks. "Hey, Cruiser you see that? Yeah you see it, I bet you can smell it too; there've been thousands of dromis over that one spot of land, but they ain't here now. This is the old Imperial Highway, Cruiser! We're making good progress. Good girl, yeah."

Gantsch was a wanderer. Many different individuals from various cultures in surprisingly diverse regions of the world had commerce with him, knew of him, had met him, had slept with him, yet it seemed no one knew where he came from. Sometimes he would tell long stories about things he had experienced or reports he had heard, but he somehow never seemed to tell anything that directly related to himself: who his parents were, what he did for a living, who he had been in love with five years ago in some faraway land. He did a little trading, sometimes, but he was not much of a merchant. He stayed with the nomads, sometimes, but he did not follow their seasonal migration routes, and he rarely stayed in any one place longer than two months.

I had lived in the same neighborhood in Kiranesh for my whole life. Then I went away, to the University in Varum; and that scholastic experience changed my life; but not so much as the journey home overland with my buddy Sriaugh, when we met a tribe of Dimpai nomads because our dromi died. What a strange series of events!

I guess I had vaguely assumed that I would marry someone from the University, because that seemed to be what people like me were expected to do. During my school years, I mated with several of the nice young ladies I met there, but I had lost all hope of ever meeting the right female for me. When I met Balhudailadishtarya, nobody had ever been so nice to me. I just wanted to keep her; but she was from the free-spirited Dimpai tribe who called themselves the Smyrna: and the only way to keep her was to leave her. So here I am, traveling the desert alone, running errands, fetching Omasu from Scruggs, and getting eaten alive... He caught himself before he allowed his train of thought to actually complain about his circumstances. *And I am so fortunate to have the opportunity,* he reminded himself adamantly.

My beautiful wife awaits me, back at the renovated capital building that was once the palace of the warlord Kragston. In a crazy twist of fate, the dead warlord's former territory is now ruled over by her mother, Quithtar. There at the compound Tarya lives with our children, raising them up to one day inherit the kingdom. And through it all, I am the luckiest boy who ever went to college.

And if I can survive these Buking Fiters, he thought, as another one sank its mandibles deep into his flesh, *then I will see my family again in just a few short weeks.*